Cam's Promise

Book 2, Northern States Pack

By Lee Oliver

Cam's Promise (Northern States Pack #2)

Cam's Promise is a work of fiction. Names, characters, places and incidents are either the product of the author's imagination or are used fictitiously and any resemblance to any actual persons, living or dead, events or locales is entirely coincidental.

Dedication

So many wonderful people help me get through my writing day. A huge shout out to Avril for her editing and promotional help, Phil for his humor, and Leah and Torhild for their help with my Facebook group. I couldn't imagine what a mess my life would be in without you all.

And a huge thank you to my readers. Your posts, comments, messages and emails make me smile and come up with even more story ideas. You all mean the world to me and I can never say that enough.

Thank you.

Table of Contents

Author's Note

So there is no confusion, yes a lot of you will know me as Lisa Oliver – author of the Cloverleah Pack, Alpha and Omega series, Arrowtown series, Bound and Bonded, Balance series and Stockton Wolves. The stories I write under Lee Oliver (a pen name stemming from childhood when I was known as Tea-Lee) are simply a way for me to write shorter length stories filled with ideas I enjoy.

The premise for these books are still the same. They contain men loving men, or in my case, paranormals who find their mates. No matter what happens on these pages, my characters always get their HEA.

I love writing, and even as I was writing this one, I was working on the next Cloverleah book, the next Balance book and I started a new story about dragons. My mind is filled with complex stories, scenes and my characters chatting loudly in my head. It can get quite overwhelming at times lol. The books under Lee Oliver are my opportunity to write simpler tales in a shorter format. That is the only difference.

Thank you all for your continued support.

Hug the one you love.

Lisa/Lee.

Prologue

(Epilogue from Book 1 – Ranger's End Game)

"Here you go; something towards your study expenses." Cam handed the young blond a hundred.

"You don't have to. It's not as though we did anything, and I'm not a whore. All I did was sleep on your bed while you were on the couch," the blond protested although Cam could see the need in his eyes.

"I'm not suggesting you're a whore," Cam said quickly, giving the young man a hug. "It's just, you told me about your studies and I know student life isn't easy."

"You sure?" The blond asked, but he was already slipping the bill into his pocket.

"Just remember our agreement," Cam warned.

"Never tell a living soul what went on tonight, unless someone gets pushy. Then tell them you're the best fuck

I've ever had." The blond wore a cheeky grin. "I don't mind finding out if that's true, you know."

"It ain't gonna happen, kid, now beat it. You have classes in a few hours. And yawn a couple of times for me."

The blond laughed and skipped out the door, full of the energy of youth after a good night's sleep. Cam closed the door with a sigh. He went over to his dresser and pulled out the picture he'd hidden there before his "date." It was a candid shot. Cam snapped it quickly during a job three years before and had kept it ever since.

The man in the picture was proud, an arrogant look on his lean, handsome face. His long black hair was similar to Ranger's, although there were no highlights or colorful streaks in it. His body was hidden under the long, leather trench coat the man was barely seen without, but Cam remembered every detail of their one night. The strength of the man's hands, the power of his thrusts, and the unabashed pleasure that lined the man's face as he climaxed with a roar and a bite.

"Fucking bastard," Cam said sadly, stroking the features of the man's face in the picture. "Why couldn't I be good enough for you to stay?" he stared at the picture until a beep from his watch reminded him he had things to do. "I'll see you tonight," he said, popping the picture back into its hiding place. Checking his game face in the mirror, Cam smoothed back his hair, straightened his back, plastered on a smile, and strode out of the room. With Ranger and Aiden on vacation, people were counting on him and he was proud of the fact he never let anyone down. Not even his mate.

Chapter One

Two weeks later

Cam straightened at the knock on the door; his smile firmly in place as he called out "enter." His smile widened as Ranger sauntered in, Aiden hot on his heels. "The happy honeymooners. How did your vacation go?"

"It was fun," Aiden said at the same time Ranger said, "tiring." Aiden glared at his ex-assassin mate and returned Cam's grin. "It was wonderful. We saw so many places. Ranger took me white water rafting and abseiling. It was brilliant fun."

"People, people, people. Everywhere we went there were people," Ranger slumped into the nearest chair. "This one," he waved a finger at his loving mate, "talks to everyone he sees. No one's a stranger. They all loved him to pieces. It was hell."

"I can imagine you found that impossible to deal with, what with your assassin training suggesting there were rogues behind every door, and the fact your mate is so damn cute."

"I'm not cute," Aiden blushed. "I just don't see the need to glower at everyone that comes along. Besides," he draped himself over Ranger's shoulder. "My smile hides the fact that what I really wanted to do was to rip their throats out for thinking they have a chance with my mate. All sighs, winks, twirling hair and bosoms being pushed in his face when I'm trying to eat. Ranger's lucky I opted for friendly."

"So, it's good to be home, then." Cam grinned, leaning his elbows on the desk. "Are you ready to take up the mantle of alpha and alpha mate? Can I get some time off at last?"

"Tomorrow," Ranger groaned. "Honestly, I know you've been doing an excellent job running things in the pack while we've been gone, but gods, if I have to smile at one more person...."

"Was there anything that needed attention right away?" Aiden asked. He was the most unlikely looking alpha in existence, but mating Ranger increased his confidence level tenfold. His blond curly hair shone under the lights; his shirt was tighter than it'd been when he left, indicating he had some solid meals under his belt, but it was the smile Cam noticed most of all. Aiden was happy, and underneath the manufactured grumpiness, it seemed Ranger was, too. A shaft of pain ran through Cam's heart and his grin widened – an automatic reflex.

"Let's see," he said shuffling his papers. "Most things have settled down now everyone knows you two are in charge. Newton's been keeping his eye on the bank. There doesn't seem to have been any upsets there now that dickhead Jenkins has left town. He's totally overhauled the loan system, as you asked, and a lot of people and businesses are taking advantage."

"That's good." Aiden beamed. "Business growth and people doing home improvements will mean a lot to this town. What happened with the brothel and soup kitchen?"

"The brothel has been relocated," Cam shook his head at the memory. "As requested, it's now on the outskirts of town and Mary, one of the local girls, is now running it. I've explained they'll get no more funding from us, but if she has any problems, to give us a call. Once she realized she could run the place as a business and customers were expected to pay rather than be *subsidized* by your father, she seemed a lot happier. From what I gather, the girls were barely making a living before."

"With the crap those girls put up with they need more than minimum wage," Aiden agreed. "What about the soup kitchen?"

"You will love this," Cam found the papers he was looking for. "After chatting with Newton, the bank bought one of Jenkin's old houses in your name and it's now a local homeless shelter. The place will provide meals three times a day for anyone who needs it. Newton's bringing in therapists, doctors, and you now employ three chefs whose sole job is to make sure no one in the Northern State goes hungry. Plus, there's a local job board and anyone who wants help with housing or work opportunities will find it there."

"Oh wow, isn't that great, Ranger?" Aiden clapped his hands. Cam had never seen anyone so happy about giving money away before, but then Aiden was one special alpha. "Finally, somewhere for homeless shifters to go. Thank you so much, Cam. You have no idea how much this means to me."

Ranger gave him the thumbs up and Cam could feel his cheeks heating. "On the local front, Mrs. Allen was upset because she claims the Gregor boys frightened her chickens and stopped them from laying. But as the boys were also seen harassing Jonesy down at the liquor mart at the same time, I guessed it had more to do with the fireworks her old man set off the night before."

"I swear Old Man Allen will blow himself up one day." Aiden shook his head.

"He probably will," Cam agreed, "but I've warned him about setting them off too close to livestock and other people. I also spoke to Jonesy. He clipped both boys around the ear and threatened to cut off their father from the store, so they are not likely to bother him again. From a pack perspective, I've arranged for enforcer challenges to start in three days, Friday, so you have plenty of time to recover before then. There are notices all over town and the Alphas of the other States have been advised, in case any of their members are interested in a transfer. I wasn't sure how many you were going to hire, given that Marcus and Shadow are here. Do you know how long they're staying or are they going to be sent away...?" Cam trailed off, looking at Ranger.

"I told the council, after that mess with Dominic, they need to completely overhaul their so-called Assassin policy before they ever think of starting it up again." Ranger touched the star tattoo on his face, probably unaware he'd done it. The tattoo was just one reason the council only had four assassins on their books. "Marcus already said he wasn't taking any more jobs. He and Shadow like it here. I won't be going anywhere. Being alpha mate is more than enough for me. I've sent invitations to Sean and Levi to join us; explaining what happened. I'm expecting them both within the week. The council will have to train a whole new set of assassins if they want any jobs done. None of us will be working for them anymore."

"They're definitely coming? Sean and Levi, I mean, not the council. We don't need the council sticking their noses in around here." Cam looked down at the desk, shuffling a few papers.

"Sean texted and confirmed. He should be here tomorrow or the next day. And you know Levi; he'll just turn up when he's ready." Ranger stood and stretched. "They both know this is important to me. I've told them the enforcer positions are there for the taking. I only want the best protecting my mate." His arm went around Aiden's shoulders and Aiden looked at him as though he'd hung the moon. "So, they will be here. They've never let me down before."

That's what I'm afraid of. Cam nodded, but fortunately, Aiden and Ranger were already focused on each other and nothing else. It was a wonder they made it out of the door. He looked at the papers in his hand and then laid them to one side. *I made a promise, but so did you,* he thought, rubbing over his aching chest. *How the hell do you expect me to keep mine if you don't keep yours? Surely you can't expect me to see you and still maintain this fiction between us.*

Unfortunately, knowing his mate as he did, Cam thought he would expect that and more. Strength was his mate's middle name. Closing his eyes, Cam ignored the solitary tear rolling down his cheek. He would never abandon Ranger, not now he had a mate to protect, but...*Gods, why does life have to be so hard?*

/~/~/~/~/

High on a hill, on the outskirts of the Northern States pack territory, a solitary figure sat staring into the fire. Flames highlighted harsh features. Long black hair, a squared chin, and eyes as black as night. A hard man. The type anyone would back away from even without the star tattoo on his face. The man had no illusions about how he looked. He didn't care. In his mind's eye, all he could see was his mate's handsome face; endlessly reliving the way the joy slipped from his features as he'd made his ruthless demands on that fateful night. *No contact. Tell no one. Promise me.*

And Cam kept that promise. The man closed his eyes but even then, all he could see was the man he'd only held once. One night. One night when the tension became unbearable and he succumbed to a moment of weakness. One bite, taken in the heat of passion – something he'd wanted to do from the moment he'd first scented Cam and now….

"Gods, I'm a five-star bastard." The man kicked a log of wood towards the fire. He'd been so arrogant back then; so certain that all he had to do was walk away and Cam would be forgotten like the countless others that had sat on his dick before. The joke was on him. He hadn't forgotten;

he couldn't forget and the pull to return, to see his mate again, was bad enough at the best of times. Now, this close to where he knew Cam was living, it was nigh impossible to ignore.

"Ranger, you canny sod. I wonder if you know, but no, I'm sure you don't. Cam kept his promise or you'd be on my ass trying to kill me." The man pulled out his phone, scrolling to the last message he'd received from one of his oldest friends.

Dominic's in jail. Huge council shake-up. Found my mate and our new home. Enforcer job waiting for you, no questions asked. It's time for you to join us. I need you, my friend.

"Fuck." The man sighed, running his hand over his face. He and Ranger, they'd trained together, trusted each other like brothers. They even worked together on occasion and it was on one of those occasions he'd met Cam, Ranger's faithful spotter. Oh, nothing happened that night, or the next dozen times the men met up on various jobs over the years. But he knew and Cam knew and one night…. "I should never have walked away."

Leaning back on the damp grass, he stared up at the stars thinking about how useless hindsight could be. Not a day went past that he hadn't thought of his mate. Hadn't wished he could turn back time; gone back to the best night of his life and treated his mate with the respect and caring he deserved.

His wolf bristled inside, tired of the restraints put on him. He knew what he wanted and the man hadn't shifted in ages because his animal was angry enough to track down and take what he wanted. "What I want too," the man said out loud, acknowledging his animal spirit for the first time since that night. "We're mates and my mate kept his promise. He can be trusted with my other secret, too. I have to believe that. I've got to believe that...." *Because the alternative?*

The man refused to think like that. Not when he was so close; not when he knew that one of the rooms in the mansion he was watching held the sleeping form of his mate. Dawn was approaching and the man needed to sleep. Tomorrow, he'd freshen up, pack his things and head down to the alpha house to answer Ranger's summons. What happened after that was entirely in the hands of his beloved mate, Cam. The man's name stayed on his lips as he fell into sleep.

Chapter Two

"So, I was thinking about going on holiday," Cam said, trying to keep his voice casual. Ranger and Aiden were enjoying a late breakfast and while he didn't think he could keep anything in his stomach, he joined them when asked, sipping on his sixth cup of coffee for the day.

"You had one not that long ago, right?" Ranger raised an eyebrow. "Something hot and sexy waiting for you in the Western States?"

"No." Lying between shifters just wasn't possible. Which made Cam's job all the more difficult. "It's just, you two have come home; you have Sean and Levi joining you in the next couple of days. I thought it might be time for me to have a wee break of my own. Aiden was so enthusiastic about white water rafting, I thought I'd give it a go. You did say the people are friendly." He winked at Aiden making Ranger growl.

"You will stay until after the enforcer challenges, won't you?" Aiden's puppy dog eyes were impossible to ignore. "You've done all the organizing already, and honestly, I haven't got a clue how to run one of these things."

"Well, I was hoping…."

Ranger cut in. "You've been a huge help and after running this pack on your own you deserve a break. But if you can hold off just a few more days and get these challenges under way. Sean and Levi should have shown up by then and we'll all muddle along until you get back."

Cam knew when he was beaten. "Sure, not a problem." He stood up and collected his half empty coffee cup. "I'll be in my office if you need me for anything."

Ranger's voice stopped him before he made it down the hallway. "Cam, you okay? You're not your usual…you know, smiley self."

"Smiley self?" Cam's grin was automatic. "Being with Aiden is softening you, old man. You'd better watch yourself or before you know it you'll be tickling babies under their chin and making silly noises at them."

"I have to do that already. Joys of being the alpha mate." Ranger sighed. "Did we do the wrong thing coming here?"

"What the hell?" Cam was shocked. He thought Ranger and Aiden were happy. "You fell for Aiden the moment you saw him and I bet you were drooling over this house the first time you came up the driveway. You've always talked about owning a house like this and having a mate is the icing on the cake."

"I know, but...." Ranger looked back down the hallway to the kitchen. "I adore my mate, you know I do, but it's like every time we step out of the freaking house, he's surrounded by people. I used to hide between jobs for a reason. This fucking tattoo has got a lot to answer for."

Despite his own worries, Cam could understand and empathize with his friend. One of the personality traits that made Ranger a perfect assassin was also the biggest barrier to him living a normal life. It wasn't so much the tattoo on his face, although that didn't help, because it signaled to anyone who came within ten feet of him that Ranger was a trained killer. But in a world where shifters everywhere looked to the strongest among them as mating material, Ranger was a target no matter where he went.

"Maybe you should start going shirtless, or at least wear clothes that clearly show your mating mark," he suggested. "Everyone knows a mated shifter can't get hard for anyone else. It might help reduce the amount of attention you are getting."

"They don't seem to care," Ranger slammed his fist into the wall beside

Cam's head denting the plaster. "They press in, always trying to get closer – I don't know if it's to me or Aiden, but either way, my wolf just wants to drop his fangs and take a chunk out of everyone. Do you know, some silly wolf shifter while we were on holiday, tried to suggest I jack off into a cup so she could use my spunk? What's wrong with these people?"

Covering his lower face with his hand, Cam coughed to hide his laughter. "How's Aiden taking all this?"

"He says it doesn't bother him, but fuck it, all I want to do is take him to a cave somewhere and growl at anyone who comes near. I'm not sure how much more I can take. I'm not used to living in a pack."

"Aiden didn't ask for this either," Cam reminded him quietly. "He didn't know his grandmother named him alpha or that his father and brothers were shits ripping off his money and freeloading in his house. But that little half-pint gets up every day and faces the world, even though I'm sure he's terrified and he does it because you're by his side."

"I know. I know. He's fucking amazing." Ranger ran his hand over his face. "When it comes down to it, he's far stronger than I'll ever be. I just wish these 'people' wouldn't take up so much of his time."

"It's a learning curve for all of us. What you need to do is set boundaries. Make sure you and Aiden have time off. A couple of days a week, maybe, or even a couple of hours a day. You are the alpha pair. If you want to schedule meetings and visits and things like that to certain hours of the day, you can. No one can stop you."

"I thought an alpha pair had to be available to their pack members at all times. That's why not many people want the job."

"That may have been how other alphas do it, but it's not like you haven't got back up. Marcus and Shadow can be available when you aren't. Marcus is an alpha, too. And in a few days, you will have the other assassins here as well. Use them. This is our new home and...." Cam broke off as there was a heavy pounding on the door and then two familiar faces strode in.

"Levi. Sean. You made it, you pair of reprobates. What do you think of our new home?" Ranger beamed, opening his arms wide.

"I'll be in my office if you need me," Cam said quietly, edging out of the hall. "Hi, guys." He managed a wave and then sprinted towards the administration wing of the house. *What the fuck? I thought I had two more days. It's too soon, too soon. I can't do this.* As soon as he was in his office, he slammed the door shut, sinking to the floor, his back against the door.

I thought I had more time. I thought I'd be away from here by now. I thought.... Cam didn't know what to think. One flash of that well-loved face and his brain ached with memories of love and the grief that came with it. His wolf was howling at him to go back. His cock, which had remained dormant for months was trying to worm its way out of his jeans. His heart was pounding and he was shaking so hard he was making the door rattle. *I can't keep my promise!* He wailed to himself. Finally giving in to the emotions that had tormented him for months, Cam fell to the floor and cried.

Chapter Three

"You have no idea how happy I am you're here," Ranger said, striding over and shaking Levi's and Sean's hands. "Maybe now the fair ladies in this pack will stop looking to me to impregnate them."

"Ha, ha," Sean slapped Ranger on the back. "What's wrong with your faithful sidekick? He ran out of here like the hounds of hell were after him. I know we've been gone a while, but I don't look that bad, do I?" He stroked his long dark beard which stood as a stark contrast to his shaven head.

"You need to leave him alone," Levi warned. "Ranger, there's something...."

"Oh, there you are, babe. Who's this? More guys sent to kill me? Haven't they got the memo I'm under your protection yet?" A beaming, curly haired blond angel sauntered in and Ranger visibly melted.

"Aiden," he said, holding out his arm. "Come and meet the last of my brother assassins. They'll form part of your inner circle. The bald one is Sean and the one who could pass as my twin without the additional hair color is Levi. Guys, I want you to meet the most important person in this territory, Aiden Chalmers, Alpha of the Northern Territories, and before anything smart comes out of your mouth, Sean, he's my fated mate."

"Pleased to meet you both." Aiden shook hands with a smile. "I know I don't look much like an Alpha, but Ranger is the brawns of this outfit. I'm just here to sign the checks and look pretty."

"Don't go running yourself down, precious. You've done more good for this territory in a month than your old man did in years." Ranger pulled Aiden close and kissed him hard enough to leave a blush.

"Ranger, man. Who'd have thought it? You're positively domesticated." Sean laughed.

"I can still beat you." Sean gulped as a long knife appeared at his throat. The funny thing was, Ranger was still holding Aiden as though he was special. "My skills have become sharper since this man agreed to be mine, not duller, and don't you forget it."

"Perfectly fine by me. Truth be told, I'm jealous," Sean said as Ranger put his knife away. "So, when do we get the grand tour? I presume we'll be staying here? And what's the guts about the council, man? I have to admit I've been off the grid for a bit."

"Ranger, I need to talk to you. Urgently. Alone." Levi hissed.

Ranger must have realized he was serious because after giving Aiden another smooch on the cheek he said quietly, "Can you show Sean around? I think Marcus and Shadow are out on the grounds. I'm sure they'll be happy to fill Sean in on what's been going on. I'll talk to Levi and we'll meet you in your office. Is that okay?"

"Sure, babe." Aiden stood on tip toes and gave Ranger another kiss. "Okay, Sean. Grab your bags. This is the main living room. Through there is the kitchen. Over here we have…." Aiden and Sean disappeared.

"Come into the Alpha office." Ranger disappeared down another hallway. Levi followed, his guts churning more than that time when he'd faced five drugged up bear shifters. Ironic how death was a possible outcome in both cases.

/~/~/~/~/

"What's this about?" Ranger leaned against the large oak desk, his arms folded, his legs crossed at the ankle. The pose, although intimidating, helped settle Levi's nerves. It was familiar, unlike the soppy love fest he'd witnessed moments before.

"Cam is my true mate." Levi straightened his spine.

Ranger's frown deepened. "Cam, as in my best friend Cam? My spotter? The guy who's saved my neck a hundred times? That Cam?"

"Yes."

"I see." Ranger swapped his feet over and Levi tensed. "You're both over the age of consent. Have been for decades. You've known him for years. When did you realize this wonderful news?" His voice suggested it was anything but.

"The first time I saw him." Levi could still remember it as though it was yesterday. Caught in a forest waiting out some rogues, Cam was covered in mud; his bright blue eyes the only color on his splattered face.

"And you've taken until now to ask permission to claim him? What kind of an ass are you?" Ranger's voice was clipped and harsh.

Levi tilted his chin. "I've already claimed him. Nine months ago, on that last job you and I did together."

"You fucking bastard!" Before Levi knew what was happening, Ranger had him pinned to the door. He could easily break his friend's hold, but the knife pressed hard against his throat made him pause.

"You knew you and Cam were mates for fucking years and never said anything?" Ranger hissed. "Then you had the audacity to fuck him, bite him, and then left him like he was one of your back-alley fucks?"

"I didn't think...."

"You had no fucking right. He's under my protection. He's always been under my protection. You violated him and probably broke his fucking heart and then you saunter in here like it was nothing?"

"It was consensual."

"Of course, it was. You're mates. He'd never say no to you. Did you let him bite you back?"

Levi closed his eyes. Of course, he didn't. Oh, he stayed faithful. His wolf wouldn't have it any other way, but there was no way anyone would know he was claimed. Except for Cam.

"I knew you'd be angry...."

"You do not put this on me!" The knife in Levi's throat dug deeper. "Cam is a beta wolf. He'd have done whatever you said. What happened? Did you force him not to tell anyone? Did you make him promise to keep your sordid secret as if you were ASHAMED OF HIM?"

"We're assassins!" Levi opened his eyes, his hands finding purchase on Ranger's chest, pushing him and the lethal looking knife away. "You depended on him every job you did. He had your back. Do you think I'd take that away from you? Allow you

41

to be killed just because I couldn't control myself?"

Shock etched itself deeply on Ranger's face. "You did this for me?"

"We're brothers from different mothers. We trained together. We swore an oath to protect each other." Levi struggled to explain. He'd spent months in seclusion, refusing contact with anyone, trying to come to terms with what he'd done. "I know you can handle yourself, but Cam's always been with you. You've never gone on a job without him. You two grew up together for fuck's sake. I wasn't about to make him choose."

"No." Ranger's snarl was back. "Instead, you made the choice for him. As if he didn't have two brain cells to rub together. In the process, he's lied to all of us; putting on his playboy act when it's plainly obvious now his dick would never harden for anyone but you. I don't know how the hell he did it, but he shouldn't have had to. You should have talked to me about this the first time you knew."

"I thought I could control myself." Levi shook his head at how stupid that idea sounded now. "It's not as though we were out in the field together much anyway. Most of our jobs were solo. I didn't want to take him as a mate. I didn't need the distraction."

"You are a true bastard in every sense of the word," Ranger said scornfully as he twirled his knife expertly through his fingers. Levi knew one wrong word and that knife would be forming a new hole between his eyes. "Cam has never deserved to be treated as though he doesn't matter. To think my brother in arms, the man I trusted...fuck, you disgust me!"

Levi couldn't disagree. In a world where mates were revered, cherished above all others, he'd put Cam in an untenable position. He'd have no one to blame but himself if the man never spoke to him again. "I came back. I came when you called. Your text said this could be our new home; that there was a job for me. I had hoped...I've never had a home. I had nothing to offer Cam before except a life of roaming from place to place with the threat of violence around every corner. I came back because you offered the type of future Cam deserves. A stable home. Not having to worry about being killed every day. A chance to build a life with my mate without endangering my brother. Was I wrong to come? Do you want me to leave?"

"If I told you to go, would you take Cam with you?"

"If that's what he wanted. I would talk to him before I went. I've taken enough decisions away from him already as you so rightly pointed out. But I won't force him to choose between us now, the same as I didn't then."

"You're still blaming my existence for your behavior. He's your mate, damn it, and my best friend. If you'd told me, I would have wanted him to be happy. How the hell can you be so cavalier about this? How long are you going to kid yourself that walking away is an option? I'd have to be dead before I left Aiden."

"I don't want to walk away. I want him in my life." Levi gave in to a moment of weakness. "Do you have any idea what it's been like? I've known he was my mate for years. It wasn't so bad before. I convinced myself we were better off apart. But since claiming him," Levi closed his eyes, a ragged groan forcing itself from his throat. "It's been a living hell. I don't dare shift. I can't be near people. I cut myself off from everyone. When I got your text, for the first time I had hope that he and I might work. Don't you understand?"

Maybe mating softened Ranger somehow. Maybe having a new home and position away from the assassin lifestyle really did bring Ranger the sense of peace Levi knew he'd been looking for. Whatever it was, the knife was now hidden and Ranger offered a twisted grin. "I don't imagine the reunion you were hoping for is going to happen for a while. Cam asked for a holiday just this morning and now I know why. You're lucky we've got the enforcer challenges coming up or you'd have missed him. I'm sure his bags were already packed and I'm guessing you're the reason."

"I don't know how he's going to feel seeing me again." Levi shrugged. "This relationship shit is like a foreign language to me. How in Fenrir's name did you manage to hang onto yours? Gossip on the council forum mentioned you'd killed two Chalmers brothers."

"I did because they were trying to kill my mate. Aiden was there, he saw it all, and while he didn't exactly cheer about it, we've gotten past it. It's a long story and one I'm sure we'll share soon enough. But for now, you have more important things to worry about. Luigi's in town does an amazing meal and it's intimate enough to provide the perfect venue for a first date."

"Date." Levi gulped. "I can do that."

"Picnics are another good idea; making sure you take the time to listen to your mate and be understanding of their moods, that's another one."

"Where did you get all this crap?"

"I'd watch what you were calling crap," Ranger laughed. "All this advice came from Cam and believe me, it works. Aiden and I are really happy. I even took him on vacation."

"You? On vacation. I'd pay big money to see that." Levi looked towards the door. His wolf let him know his mate was nearby. "Can I go and talk to

Cam, or did you want to speak to him first?"

"You can let him know that I understand why he did what he did and I don't hold any grudges against him. Cam's loyal to a fault. His deception with me will have devastated him. I hope you understand just how much damage your selfish actions have done. Trust is everything in our game and you know it."

"I trusted Cam."

"And he didn't break that trust, so whatever shit he throws at you, you take it." Ranger stepped closer and Levi was reminded of why Ranger was the best at what they did. "You only get one chance. Break his heart again and I'll fucking end you myself. You hear me?"

"Understood." Levi felt as though a huge weight lifted from his shoulders. "So, can I track him down?"

"Good luck with that. You've got until noon Friday to make things right. The enforcer challenge is then and Cam's the one running it."

"Will I be fighting for my position?"

"Nah, neither will Marcus or Sean. No point in scaring off the potentials before they've got their shirts off. Unless someone makes a big deal about it, in which case you can show them what you're made of." Ranger looked up and his grin widened as the door opened and Aiden walked in. "Go. Good luck. Don't forget Luigi's and remember what I said."

Levi disappeared out the same door while Ranger and Aiden were busy sucking faces. *Gods, I can't wait to have a relationship like that.*

Chapter Four

Tired after his emotional outpouring, nonetheless, Cam knew he had a job to do. The manual from the council regarding enforcer challenges was clear and he was on the phone with a local contractor trying to get the challenge circle built in time when he heard a knock at the door. Figuring it was probably Ranger wanting to talk to him some more about his own problems, Cam yelled "come in" before giving his attention back to the phone.

"I really don't care what the last alpha did or didn't do," he said firmly. "Aiden Chalmers is the alpha now and he's holding enforcer challenges. Just because Joe Blow's father, brother, and distant cousin used to work as enforcers for the elder Chalmers, they clearly didn't have Aiden's back. If they want to be considered, then they need to fight the same as everyone else."

His eyes widened and his heart began to beat a path to his cock as he watched Levi saunter in, quietly closing the door. "I said I don't care," his words were more forceful as he cut off the whining contractor. "Either you get your ass into gear and do the job, or you and your family can pack your bags and get out of this territory. Aiden's already done a lot of good for this area and I'm sure it won't be hard to find someone else who can do a simple job without bad-mouthing him behind his back."

"I didn't mean no disrespect, sir. I'll get my boys..." The contractor was groveling now but Cam was having trouble breathing. Seeing Levi, his long hair, muscled chest, and thighs outlined perfectly by worn jeans was more than his heart could take. The casual way he sank into the chair in front of the desk; the way he lifted his hair from his neck. The air was quickly saturated with the scent that sent all Cam's senses reeling. After getting assurances the job would be done Cam disconnected the call.

"Levi." It was all he could manage. After years of dreaming, months of hoping, to see him now in the flesh was more than Cam could bear. "You don't have to worry," he forced himself to continue as he saw Levi's jaw harden. "No one knows. I kept my word. I won't let you down. I'll be gone in a few days and I'm sure I can stay out of your way until then." Actually, Cam had no idea how he would keep that promise, but then, like all the other things he held close to his chest, he knew he'd find a way. He would do anything it took to make his mate happy.

"I spoke to Ranger." Levi's voice was like gravel, as though he hadn't spoken for a while.

"You're not staying?" Cam didn't know why his heart suddenly felt as though it'd been split in two. It wasn't as though there was much left of his poor battered organ to start with. "Of course, I understand, but why?" *Why hunt me down in my office? Why turn up if you were only going to leave again? Why fucking force me to watch you go out that door a second fucking time?*

"I'm staying. I just had to clear a few things with Ranger first."

"Okay, right." *Probably council business.* Cam busied himself with the papers on his desk. "I'll be sure to stay out of your way. Was that all you wanted to tell me?"

"Cam." The use of his name forced him to look up. "I'm staying."

Cam gulped and dropped his eyes again; his papers were easier to look at than the intensity of Levi's eyes. "Yes, so you said and that's fine...good...Ranger was worried about protection for Aiden. He'll be glad you're here. I'll...I have to stay for a couple of days, I promised Ranger, but after that, I'll be out of your hair."

He had no idea where he was going to go. He'd been with Ranger his entire adult life. *The far end of the Southern territory might be the best idea.* Because seeing Levi, smelling him, having him close enough to touch; Cam's defenses were crumbling faster than an ice cream on a hot plate. He clung to the underneath of his desk, hoping that would be enough to stop him flying over the desk and slamming his mate to the ground. Those full lips, those dark eyes...Cam jumped when he realized Levi was talking again.

"I'm clearly not very good at this. When I said I was staying, I meant I wanted to stay with you. I want us to be mates. I've cleared it with Ranger...."

"You told Ranger you claimed me?" Cam's eyes roved over Levi's body for a completely different reason this time. Apart from a narrow red mark on his neck, he seemed fine. "Are you trying to get yourself killed? He was the reason you didn't want me in the first place."

"He was one of the reasons." Levi sighed. "There's a lot you don't know about me; things I will tell you in time, but please," Cam couldn't remember ever hearing that word come from Levi's lips. "Will you give us a chance?"

Cam's hands left the desk and his feet pushed hard on the floor as he leaped out of his chair, crashing into Levi's. They fell with a thud, the chair splintered but Cam was in heaven. He buried his nose in Levi's neck; deep breaths taking in the smell of oak moss and basil underlined with the heady scent of leather coming from Levi's long coat. His cock hard, he humped and writhed, not even realizing his hands were clutching Levi's shoulders until the man moved.

"Don't," he whispered, terrified he was about to be dumped on the floor. "My wolf." Cam's wolf was in a frenzy of excitement, running around, chasing his tail, yelping like a pup. Cam understood. Levi was the stronger shifter, he was their mate, and the way Cam's wolf grieved when they were left was heartbreaking. A strong hand fluttered in his hair and then pressed down, pushing Cam's nose where it wanted to be. He groaned and rubbed his face up Levi's neck and jaw then pulled back.

"I'm sorry," he whispered unable to meet Levi's eyes. "I didn't mean to scent mark you." He tried to pull away but the hand on his head and the one on his ass didn't give him anywhere to move. All of a sudden, he was conscious of Levi's heaving chest and the cloth covered ridge nudging his cock. Peering up, he saw his mate's eyes swamped with lust. "Oh." Cam pushed down with his hips and Levi bit his lip. "Double Oh." Leaning slightly to one side, Cam fumbled with zippers and belts, a gasp escaping his lips as first Levi's and then his cock hit the air. He shoved Levi's shirt up and then rolled back down. He couldn't stop humping if his life depended on it.

"I won't last."

"Me neither." Arching his back slightly Cam pushed down again. His head was tilted and suddenly Levi's lips were bruising his. *Our first kiss.* That thought alone was enough to send his cock spurting and seconds later Levi's body went rigid as his mate came. But Levi didn't let loose his hold, and now the initial urgency had passed, Cam could focus on the softness of Levi's full lips; his chin rubbed raw by Levi's closely-groomed facial hair. Fisting his hands in Levi's locks, Cam hung on for the ride.

/~/~/~/~/

Levi didn't realize how much he was starving for his mate's touch until Cam landed on top of him. His wolf snarled, eager to sink his fangs into his mate's flesh, but Levi pushed him back. He was in the middle of his first ever kiss and nothing was going to stop him from tasting every inch of Cam's mouth. His tongue, his gums, Levi even ran his tongue over Cam's white teeth. His hands were gripped on Cam so tight, his knuckles cracked. Even the knowledge he was leaving bruises wasn't enough to make him let go.

Bruises. Marks. Cam was his and while Levi had spent a lot of years denying it, he could feel their connection hum between them as his cock hardened – *like it'd ever gone down* – and his urge to feel Cam's naked flesh increased. Claws appeared, slashing through Cam's clothing, Levi's need rising with every inch revealed. Cam's abs flexed on his belly, his cock was matching his thrust for thrust but it wasn't enough. Hoisting Cam's hips up, he tore his mate's jeans from his legs, before settling Cam over him again, his cock seeking Cam's hole.

"Lube!" Cam yelled as Levi finally hit the opening he was looking for.

Scrambling up, Cam kicked his clothes aside. Naked except for his boots, he stumbled over to his desk drawer, papers and clips cast aside in his haste.

"Yes." Cam's face was a joy to behold as he held up a tiny one-use packet before tearing it open with his teeth. Levi wanted to know what *that* was doing in his desk drawer but his growl was forgotten as Cam dropped over him, his hands fumbling behind him.

"Can't wait," Cam panted and Levi felt the brush of his hand across his cock, leaving it sticky. "Now we just have to…yes."

Cam wasn't the only one groaning as the head of Levi's cock was suddenly caught in tight heat. "Slow down. We've got time." Another new thing to add to his list. Levi never cared about partner comfort, but his brain was screaming at him that this wasn't a one-night fuck and he'd be damned if he'd treat Cam like that…again.

"Easy does it, I'm not going anywhere."

Looking up, Levi could see Cam's wolf in his eyes, the hint of fang catching his bottom lip. Feral was the only word that could be used to describe the look on his mate's face and Levi knew if Cam had been alpha born, he'd be the one trying to shove a thick length in a small hole.

All at once Cam's intensity made sense. In all the time they'd been apart, Levi had only selfishly worried about how their separation affected him. It wasn't just the human Cam he'd walked away from; it was his mate's poor animal half, too. Waiting barely long enough for his mate to be seated, he didn't want a crimp in his cock, after all, Levi pulled Cam down, slashing his t-shirt at the neck and shoving his coat collar aside. "Bite me," he grunted as he thrust his hips up. "Fucking bite me for all the world to see."

There was no hesitation. Levi felt a pinch of pain before the blood in his body exploded like a supernova. His cock pulsed mid-thrust as his orgasm hit him from nowhere and from the spurt on his belly, Cam had gone off like a rocket, too. Waiting just long enough for Cam to give one lick across a mark Levi knew would scar, Levi plunged his fangs into the pale white mark Cam wore, a groan bubbling in his throat as Levi drank.

Cam stiffened and then relaxed, and with his cock still firmly encased in the heat of his mate's body, Levi let go. For the first time with another person, he could be his true self and he felt their bond strengthen with every sip. Well before he was ready, Levi pulled away, gently licking every last drop left on Cam's skin. His mate was thinner than when they originally bonded and he made a mental note to see to it Cam ate more regularly.

"Half vampire?" Cam's voice was low but steady. "Was that what you wanted to tell me?"

Levi nodded, unsure how Cam would take the news. Hybrids weren't treated well by pure shifters as a rule.

"Is that the other reason you left?"

Levi nodded again. He could do nothing else. If Cam left him now he wouldn't last a month, which was the only reason he hadn't drunk from Cam when he originally claimed him. And *that* had been a lot more difficult than it sounded. His dual natures were equally strong.

"What does this mean for our mating?" Cam hadn't moved away, which Levi took as a positive.

"It means you are not only my mate, you are my beloved mate. From this day forward I won't be able to feed from anyone else. When I claimed you before, only my wolf teeth engaged. Now all parts of my soul are joined with yours."

"Does this mean you're going to stick around permanently this time?"

Levi hadn't realized Cam was still unsure of him. But Ranger's words rang through his brain. "I will never leave your side again. You have my word."

Cam's eyes scanned his face and Levi relaxed under the scrutiny. He was finally with someone he didn't need to hide his dual nature from.

"Does Ranger know about your blood drinking habits?"

Levi shook his head. "No one does except Dominic and Tron. Ranger's text indicated Dominic's no longer a problem for us and Tron will never tell."

"You know Ranger wouldn't care, don't you? He considers you a brother."

Levi wasn't so sure. Although Ranger was as much an outcast as he was, his friend was now alpha mate. Being with Cam now, Levi could keep his vampire side hidden behind the privacy of their bedroom door. He'd had decades of experience keeping his secrets. But he nodded because Cam seemed to expect it.

"And our relationship," Cam hung his head. "Do we have to keep hiding that too now?"

"I doubt I could keep my hands off you, no matter where we are." Levi tried smiling. From the crack in his face, as he attempted to use muscles that had lain dormant for years, he wasn't sure he was successful. "I won't hide you anymore. In fact, I'd love it if we could go out for a ride. You could show me some of the territory. It's been years since I've been here. And after that, I'd like you to come to dinner with me at Luigi's."

"You don't have to court me. I've been yours since the first time I inhaled your scent." Cam seemed embarrassed and Levi wasn't sure why.

"I haven't said sorry to you yet," Levi lowered his voice, sure his scent would indicate just how sincere he was. "While that one word won't be enough to wipe out the years of torment I've put you through, I'd like to try and show you that I mean what I say when I tell you I've never stopped wanting you."

Cam looked down. Their bellies were encrusted with drying spunk and Levi's cock was softening, which was also going to leave a mess. "We'd better think of a way of getting from here to my room so we can shower then. There's no point in my putting on my clothes again. They're only fit for the rag bin."

"You can borrow my coat, unless you want to shift?"

"Aiden's not fond of fur in the house." Cam gingerly got up. "I'll borrow your coat if you don't mind. Your jeans still seem clean."

Recognizing Cam wanted to hold onto his scent a while longer, Levi stood and shrugged off his coat, handing it over. It was heavy, it's secret pockets full of weapons but Cam pulled it on, wrapping it around him tightly. Levi draped his arm around Cam's shoulder and left it there as they went to Cam's room. They caught a few strange looks. It was clear Cam had nothing on but the coat and his boots. But Levi didn't know these people and he didn't care what they thought. He had his mate under his arm at last and it was a good feeling. One he didn't think would dissipate anytime soon.

Chapter Five

"This food is amazing." Cam grinned over his plate of pasta at Levi who was watching him eat. The afternoon had been everything he dreamed of. Levi was attentive, never let him out of his sight, and while he tensed whenever pack members came too close, he was making an effort.

After being with Ranger for so many years, Cam knew it was difficult for any of the assassins to behave like regular shifters. They tended to keep to the shadows; finding their hook ups in dingy bars in between tracking rogues and killing criminals. They rarely had friends outside their immediate small circle and none of them had family to speak of. Cam was an oddity in that he worked closely with his brother Newton. His few hours with Levi highlighted to Cam Ranger's difficulties while on vacation. Being in a pack was a totally different way of life and while Cam was able to adjust better; his beta wolf status meant he cared about people, he could understand just how hard the adaption was for Ranger and Levi.

"Ranger recommended the place," Levi laid his knife and fork neatly across the plate. "I was told he got his dating tips from you."

"He was clueless. Mind you, he met Aiden on a training camp we were running for Dominic. Long story." Cam didn't feel a bit disloyal saying what everyone else knew. "The thing is, Aiden loves him anyway. You should've seen him when he confronted his father. There he was with two dead brothers on the floor and the blood dripping from Ranger's knife. But as soon as his father was dragged off to jail, he and Ranger were busy mauling each other, uncaring who saw them."

"They seem to make a good alpha pair; not that I've got any experience with such things."

"Was it hard growing up? Did you grow up in a pack?" Cam hesitated for a moment and then reached out and put his hand on his mate's. The sensation was still new enough to send the butterflies in his stomach into a frenzy, but for all their physical attraction, Cam knew nothing about his mate at all beyond his job.

"Nope." Levi was wearing his assassin mask again and Cam wished he hadn't asked. "I was a foundling, raised in a shifter orphanage. But the other side of my nature required feeding from birth, so I was marked as different well before my face was tattooed. I ran away when I was eight, lived on the streets for about six years before I was caught by one of the council guards for shoplifting. Dragged before the council, Dominic saw potential in me and sent me to boot camp. I was a grunt for a few years until there was an altercation at the camp one day and I got sent to Tron. The assassins were the only true family I had until now."

"Shit. I am sorry." Cam's life wasn't much better, although he and Ranger had been together since they were kids. When Ranger was encouraged to go into assassin training, he refused to go unless Cam went with him. Because he was a beta wolf, Cam wasn't eligible to become an assassin himself. Not that his kill count was much below Levi's or Ranger's. He just didn't have the tattoo, pay rates, or fan fair and following that went with the assassin's position.

"Ranger must have accepted your claim on me or we wouldn't be sharing this great meal. I hope I can convince you being mated will add to your life, not take away from it. Although...." Cam swallowed, then lowering his voice, he leaned over the table. "Your feeding," he whispered. "How did you...did you ever...after you bit me...how did you...?" He felt like an ass for asking, but Cam's wolf was just as possessive as Levi's and the thought of Levi being intimate with anyone else, even for feeding purposes, had his fangs dropping and claws springing from his fingers.

"It's all right." Thank the Fates Levi seemed to understand the sudden surge of his wolf. "We'll discuss it when we get back I promise, but from the moment I claimed you I've touched no one else unless I was killing them."

"Good. That's good. I mean...." Cam shut up. He was making a fool of himself. But to him, feeding from a body couldn't be anything but an intimate act. Levi promised explanations later and Cam would hold him to that. "Are you about finished? Did you want dessert? Coffee? Another drink before we head back?"

"I think I've reached my people limit," Levi admitted. "I'll get the check." He lifted a finger and an older waitress came over with a smile. Cam could see she was another reason Ranger liked the place. It was a mom and pop restaurant and apart from a slight widening of the eyes when she first saw them together, Wendy had been polite and friendly throughout the meal.

"I have my own entrance back at the house," he said with a wink as Wendy went off to tally up the account. "We don't have to see anyone else once we get on the bike."

"That'd be...." Levi stiffened and then he sniffed. Cam looked up to see three men/wolves approaching their table; "Northern Construction" emblazoned across the front of their tight shirts.

"I think this is for me," Cam muttered. He refused to stand up as the three men crowded the table. "Yes, gentlemen. Is there anything I can do for you?"

"You're him, aren't you? The Alpha's second." The middle man spat on the floor. All three shifters were showing signs of age, which meant they were either really, really old or they didn't take care of their wolf spirit. Cam was leaning towards the latter.

"I'm Alpha Chalmers' second, yes. Is this important? As you can see, my mate and I have just finished our meal. I'm sure any complaints you have can be directed to the office in the morning."

"This won't wait. What's all this about holding enforcer challenges in the first place? The alpha should be hiring back the men his father employed when he was around. There's no need for challenges."

"Were all three of you in the previous alpha's employ?" Cam looked around. Things were about to get messy.

"Yeah, we were and we got no notification we'd been fired. We want our jobs back."

"Then you should be speaking to the alpha directly." The worried looks the three men shared suggested they didn't want to mess with Ranger.

Maybe they should have paid closer attention to his mate.

Letting out a long sigh, Cam smiled at Levi. "Excuse me please, mate. I need to handle this outside. Gentlemen?" He pointed to the door as he stood up. He didn't have time to explain the situation to Levi, as much as he'd like to. Instead, he followed the men outside, facing them as they stood in the middle of the street.

"Now then, as the previous alpha's enforcers, you were aware the position wasn't held legitimately by Mr. Chalmers at all. He was simply a regent, holding the place until Aiden came of age, right?"

Joe looked at his friends, brothers, or whoever they were and the other two shook their head.

"Do you remember Aiden's grandmother? The last true alpha of this territory?"

"No. We were brought in from the Southern territory when the elder Alpha Chalmers took over. He never said nothin about any of this shit and we don't care about it, either. We was employed to be pack enforcers and as we haven't been fired, we want to know why the hell there are notices up everywhere goin on about this bleeding challenge. Thems are our jobs."

"And yet you run a construction company?" Cam waved at the shirts the men were wearing. "Any enforcer worth his salt knows the job is full time. Where were you three when the Alpha Regent was arrested? There were no enforcers in the house when he was taken."

Joe shrugged. "He didn't need us around. It ain't like anyone would challenge him anyways. No one dared. Those were our jobs and we want 'em back. I got a letter from the bank today tellin' me I had to start payin' on the house I'm in. My kin got them too. Those houses are part of our pay package."

"Not anymore." Cam flexed his shoulders. "The way I see it, you have three options. One, you can challenge for a position." Cam was sure they wouldn't be successful. "Two, you can continue with your construction work and make payments on your houses just like any other citizen who chooses to live in the Northern State territory or three, you can leave the territory with the same rights and conditions as everyone else here."

"Or, we can challenge you for your position and then no one can kick us out anywhere."

And this was why Cam wanted out of the restaurant. There was no way Luigi's was going to be trashed simply because some bigots hadn't learned to work with the change in command. Waiting just long enough for Joe to throw the first punch, he fought back; kicking one guy in the nuts as he slammed a solid punch into Joe's stomach. The damaged nut guy sank to the ground with a groan, cupping his groin, but the third man grabbed him from behind. Cam was used to being ganged up on. Using the man's body weight as leverage, he kicked up and caught Joe's neck between his calf muscles, pulling him down with a satisfying clunk on the bitumen. Suddenly, the man holding him was gone and Cam turned to see Levi tossing him to the ground.

"I had it handled," Cam panted. Joe groaned and stirred and he quickly kicked the man in the head. "It was a challenge fight."

"Challenges are done one on one. Every shifter in existence knows to interfere with a challenge is an automatic forfeit. I should kill them all." Levi was pissed. If his clenched fists weren't proof enough, his fangs and blazing eyes definitely were. Noticing they'd garnered an audience, Cam pulled out his phone.

"Ranger," he said cheerfully when his call was answered. "We need to transport three to the brig. They're fans of Aiden's dear old dad and got pissed off about the enforcer challenges. We're outside Luigi's."

"On my way."

Cam pocketed his phone. He'd preferred if Marcus and Shadow had come. It would've been better if he could've transported them himself, but they had taken Levi's bike.

"Sorry about the date, lover," he grinned at Levi, trying to break some of the tension. Levi had all three men trussed up like Thanksgiving turkeys. Cam wondered where he got the rope until he saw Luigi scowling at the three men.

"You guys are no good for our town." Luigi snarled at Joe who was frowning at the crowd. "Our Alpha is good now and you had to come and cause trouble. Stupid. Stupid people don't eat my food." He flicked the guys off and stalked back into the restaurant.

"One more tip in how to win friends and influence people." Cam saw Ranger's Lamborghini flying down the road with his SUV following behind. "Okay, people. Can you stand back and let the alpha and alpha mate through, please? Let's get this shit off the road so we can enjoy the rest of our evening."

A few of the crowd laughed and they cleared the road, allowing Ranger to pull his car to a screeching stop, complete with tire smoke.

"What happened. Who are these bastards?" Ranger looked Cam up and down, probably making sure he was all right. Cam was more worried about Levi, who was standing statue still, his arms crossed. Cam wanted to go to him; wrap his arms around him and inhale his scent, but with that look on Levi's face, he didn't dare.

"Previous enforcers," he answered Ranger. "They're upset because they lost their jobs without warning, so challenged me for mine."

"You won three challenges?" Ranger looked impressed and Cam didn't want to let him down, but he had to be honest.

"More like a three on one deal. Levi intervened after I put two of them down. Seemed only fair, seeing as the challenge was void the moment that one caught hold of me so that one," Cam pointed, "could punch the shit out of me."

"I won't have brawling in this town." Aiden frowned. "This is the business area, there could have been children here. If anyone wants to fight, that's what the challenge circle is for."

"Yeah, well, they were the guys who were supposed to build that, too," Cam sighed. "I'll get Newton to go through the pay records and see how many other people have been paid for work they're not doing. After I've found a new contracting firm to set up the challenge circle." Damn it. He could see his time with Levi slipping away.

"We can build the challenge circle." Two young men from the crowd stepped forward. "I'm Kyle and this is my brother Michael. We used to work construction here before these guys threatened our business. All we've been able to pick up is the odd job and we could do with the money. You have my word we'll do a good job."

"Add intimidation to these guy's charges." Cam nodded at Kyle. "You've got the job. It must be finished by Friday morning. I'll pay you double your going rate if you get it done on time."

"Thank you, sir," Kyle showed his neck. "You too, Alpha, Alpha Mate." The poor guy was going to get a crick in his neck.

"Come and see me in the office tomorrow. At the pack house." Cam turned away but not before he caught Kyle and Michael hugging each other and doing a happy dance in the street. He grinned. It was a nice feeling doing something for others.

Marcus and Shadow had gotten out of the SUV and were loading up the prisoners. Cam walked over to Levi and hesitantly laid his hand on the man's arm.

"You okay?"

"You could have been hurt," Levi whispered but Cam didn't have time to reply. His feet left the ground and his mouth was being ravaged by Levi's lips. *Okay, so that expression is worry, not anger. Must remember that* Cam thought as he went limp in Levi's arms and let him have his way.

Chapter Six

Levi never imagined the bond between them could be so intense. Sure, his wolf hated him when he walked away from Cam after claiming him the first time, but his vampire half was a perfect counterbalance, preaching patience and sensibility. Levi hadn't wanted to upset Ranger and he wasn't sure enough of Cam to tell his secret. But now both halves of his inner self were firmly on the "protect Cam at all costs" wagon and Levi's nerves were stretched to breaking point. How could he not have guessed Cam would be pack second if Ranger was Alpha Mate? The pack second - a job that came with challenges, fights, and danger.

You've seen him fight before. You're on the main street for fuck's sake. Levi didn't care. Cam was in his arms, his legs wrapped around his waist and he was taking all of Levi's harsh attentions like a champ. Both wolf and vampire needed to claim him and for a moment, Levi couldn't think of a single reason why he needed to hold back.

"Levi!" Oh, that was why. Ranger was on one side of him, Marcus on the other. Levi wrenched his mouth from Cam's long enough to snarl. No one was getting near his mate.

"Don't mind them, they're newly mated. Can't keep their hands off each other." Levi heard Aiden's laughter following his words and guessed that was for the crowd's benefit. Meanwhile, Marcus and Ranger had him firmly gripped by his biceps, moving him towards the SUV.

"You put me in that wagon and those prisoners will be dead before we get back to the pack house. I'm not having them near Cam again."

"You can't fuck Cam on the street, either. Do you want people seeing him naked?" At least Shadow thought it was funny, but Levi didn't. No one was allowed to see his mate's delicious body in the throes of passion.

"We'll take the bike." Ranger's claws left scratch marks in the leather of his coat as he pulled away; Levi would take that out of his hide later. For now, he had a hot and panting mate in his arms and a cock threatening to burst the seams of his pants.

"I'm okay," Cam whispered against his cheek. "A few bruises, maybe a scrape or two, but I do know how to look after myself."

"Don't push me on this now." Levi stared at his bike. He was going to have to put Cam down and neither side of his personality was pleased.

"You can bet we're going to talk about this later." Cam landed on his feet with a thump. "Get on the bike." He crossed his arms and waited.

Be understanding of his moods, Levi remembered Ranger's advice. *Aargh. More like bullshit relationship crap.* He climbed on and got the bike started, barely waiting for Cam to be seated before he took off down the road.

He's got no reason to be shitty with me. He could've been hurt. Levi's mind supplied him with graphic images of Cam beaten and maimed. Lifeless eyes staring back at him like so many had before. He closed his eyes and then they flew open again as the bike jolted. Spying a stand of trees, he pulled over, uncaring of how the rough ground would affect the bike's suspension. Turning off the key, he leaned forward on the handle bars, breathing heavily.

"Levi. Levi, what's wrong?" Cam's hand was warm on his shoulder.

"My fucking dual nature." Sitting up, he swung his leg over the handle bars, jumping to the ground. He needed distance. He needed words. "Have you ever come across a vampire when you were working with Ranger?"

"A few times." Cam seemed relaxed enough now and at least he stayed on the bike. "Not often. The shifter council usually passes on complaints about vampires to the vampire council. But yeah, I've come across a few. Vicious bastards when they're angry. Is that what's wrong with you? You're angry at me?"

"Yes. No." Levi shook his head. "No. I'm not angry *with you*. It's hard to explain. You have your wolf nature. You're a beta wolf. You fight, you care for the safety of the pack, and you love with your whole heart when you share it."

"It's my nature. It's the way I was born to be."

"Exactly and you're perfect the way you are." Levi wasn't sure what part of his nature pushed those words out of his mouth, but they made Cam smile so he'd take that as a win. "My nature is different. I am Alpha wolf which means I'll protect my mate till my last breath, but I'm also overbearing."

Cam coughed and might have said something but Levi chose to ignore it.

"The vampire half of me is hellishly strong. As strong, if not more, than my wolf side. He's also smart, quick to anger but highly controlled when it comes to emotions. When I first met you, it was my wolf who wanted the claim. After my wolf claimed you, it was my vampire who gave me the strength to walk away."

"Your vampire half doesn't accept me as his beloved?"

You're being an asshole. Stop upsetting him. "Vampires don't know for sure someone is their beloved until they've fed from them. When my wolf half claimed you, I refused to swallow any of your blood. My wolf wanted the mark and I was powerless to stop him. You have to remember, at the time, I thought Ranger would kill me, and I didn't know you'd accept my hybrid status," Levi added when he saw he was upsetting Cam more. "I just couldn't help myself. Being around you that last time...I lost control."

"Nice to know your wolf side gets a say in some things." Levi was sure he saw Cam's lips twitch.

"That was before. My wolf has always seen and wanted to protect you as a mate. My vampire side was cautious, but now he's claimed you, too. Then you got into a fight and my dual nature ganged up on me. I knew you could handle yourself. My spirits know it too, but they still wanted to kill everyone in a ten-foot radius of us."

"Hence the mad need to fuck me in the middle of the main street. I get it. I might only be a beta wolf but your ass was looking like a steak dinner to a starving dog once the danger passed."

Really? Levi resisted the urge to look over his shoulder. He wasn't sure how to respond to that, so he ignored it. "Please understand. Anything you knew about alpha wolves goes double for me. My vampire now sees you as his sole reason for living. I can't promise I won't over react when things get tough."

"I can accept that, provided you realize I am a strong wolf in my own right." Cam slipped off the bike and came closer. "But you almost crashed the bike with me on it, and that doesn't sound protective. What happened then?"

Levi closed his eyes. "I'm a killer. I've got a lot of deaths on my conscience. I remember every one of them. That thing before...I don't know why. My brain was filled with images of you being maimed and beaten. It was three against one on that street. Then in my head, I saw you staring at me with lifeless eyes. I lost it." The last words were mumbled but Levi trusted Cam's hearing.

"I can't imagine what that must have been like." Cam's arms held him close and Levi rested his head on his mate's broad shoulder. "But you don't have to figure this out now or cope with any of this on your own. I've had a lot of experience of dealing with Ranger's drunken ass when he can't cope with the memories. At least with you, I can distract you with my naked body."

"Ranger goes through this too?"

"And Marcus, although, since he and Ranger have both mated they seem a lot more settled. I worry about Sean. But you'll find that same kind of peace once we've been together a while."

"At least my dual natures are working together now. These last months have been tough."

"I know." Cam's tone held no hint of censure but Levi mentally kicked himself.

"Did I tell you how sorry I am? I had no right to make you suffer all these years."

"I think we've both been suffering," Cam brushed his cheek and Levi melted. "But I've kept your promises for you when you asked me to. Will you keep one for me?"

"Anything." Now Levi had committed himself, he'd do anything for his mate.

"Promise me you'll never leave me or ignore what we are to each other in front of anyone else again. Please."

"You give me the easy promises to keep." Levi licked across Cam's jaw. "You have my word as a man, as a wolf, and as a vampire."

"Thank you." Cam kissed the top of his head and Levi marveled at how easy it was for his mate to be affectionate. He had a lot to learn. "So, are you ready to go back, or shall we give your wolf it's freedom and have a run while we are here?"

Levi laughed as his wolf howled. "My wolf is dying to meet yours. But step over by the bike to shift, would you? Me and my vampire can think of plenty of things to do with your naked body that doesn't involve running on four legs."

"The conflict of your dual nature," Cam laughed, but after a quick hug, he moved away and less than a minute later, a large dark brown wolf stood in his place.

/~/~/~/~/

Levi wasn't the only one who'd not shifted for a while. Cam's wolf had been just as keen to track down their errant mate as Levi's had been. So, it was with a sense of relief that Cam let his wolf side come through. Levi looked different from his four footed perspective; taller, broader, and Cam's wolf was well aware of the strength of Levi's spirits. But that didn't stop him bounding over as Levi bent to remove his boots and pants. He sniffed around while Levi removed his clothes, getting a growl for his trouble when his nose hit Levi's butt.

Oops. Cam sat back on his haunches, his tongue hanging out. Leaving his clothes in a neat pile, Levi shook his head and then shifted. It was fast. One blink and a large black wolf with dark eyes glared at him, a deep rumble emanating from his chest. Cam knew what to do. He was a good beta wolf. Crouching down, he lowered his head and waited for his alpha to approach. He couldn't do anything about his perky ears or the way he watched his alpha approach. He was happy his Alpha recognized him and barely resisted the urge to pounce on the solid wolf as he got close.

The power coming from Levi's furry form was incredible. Cam was used to Ranger, who was formidable at the best of times, but Levi was in a class of his own. Cam wasn't sure if it was because his hybrid half was so powerful or if this was all Levi's genetics but he couldn't stop a whimper escaping as Levi sniffed him over. A lick along his jaw let Cam know his mate approved of him and he bounced back up, tail wagging madly, eager to play.

For a moment, Levi hesitated. Maybe he'd never played, but then his wolf side must have given him a push and within seconds the two wolves were running, jumping, and mock fighting, rolling around in the grass together. For Cam's wolf, it was heaven.

Chapter Seven

"Hmm, you up for another round? Not that I'm complaining. I've got months of celibacy to make up for." Cam was gorgeous when he was wearing his "just been fucked" look. His blond hair was sticking up all over the place, his eyes were half closed and his mouth was twisted in a lazy smile. Levi had never seen anyone so stunning. They were in Cam's room and Levi's dual nature was finally satisfied his mate was well and truly claimed. But he felt he needed to do something else.

Swallowing hard, Levi said quietly, "I thought you could take me this time. My wolf reminded me of our manners," Cam chuckled and Levi could see the humor. Wolves weren't known for their finesse. "I've never bottomed before and I'm unlikely to do it often, but I think I need to be claimed properly. Your wolf needs it and so do I."

Cam sat up and Levi closed his eyes as a capable hand stroked his face. "It's a big deal, your first time. Are you sure you're ready for this? Not that I'm not over the moon keen, don't get me wrong. But I don't want you pushing yourself to do something you're not comfortable with because of some form of misguided guilt."

Levi knew his laugh was shaky. "It's got nothing to do with guilt and everything to do with us being equals behind our bedroom door. I've never done it. Never even considered it before. But with you, I want things to be different. I've had years to think about our mating. I want this. I want you."

"I'll do my best to make it good for you." Both of Cam's hands were framing his face now and Levi moaned into their shared kiss. Everything about Cam was strong, yet, his touch was so gentle. Tumbling back onto the mattress, Levi found himself underneath Cam and quickly calmed his wolf who wasn't keen on the position. Exhaling long and slow through his nose he pushed everything out of his mind except the feel of Cam's hands on his torso; brushing lightly over his nipples, tickling under his arms. Cam's clever tongue was following his fingers, mapping out Levi's body and his cock slapped his belly as Cam lifted his bum cheeks.

"You smell amazing," Cam moaned as his tongue slathered over Levi's balls. "You taste even better."

Levi jumped when Cam's tongue dipped into the base of his crease. *He's going to...fuck, yes, he is.* Fisting the coverlets, Levi bit his lip to stop from gasping. Back alley hook-ups never involved rimming, but fuck, Levi was ready to sign up for life. Nerve endings he didn't know he had quivered under a dexterous tongue. His cock sent the signal to thrust, but the silly thing was flapping in the air and there was no way Levi was moving away from Cam's mouth.

"Hmm, I knew it," Cam sat up, wiping the saliva from his chin. "You taste amazing. Pass me the lube?"

Lube. Shit. No matter how often guys had sex with each other there was no getting past the prep stage; something Levi knew was necessary, otherwise that length Cam was sporting would hurt. But that didn't stop him wishing Cam was already inside him, making him feel good. He handed over the battered tube, hoping they'd left enough in there. *Use lots.*

"There's no need to be nervous about this bit. I'll take it slow." Cam laid over Levi's body, kissing him hard. Levi wanted to pull away; to tell his mate not to go slow. To just shove his dick in there and get on with it. Slow meant he had time to think about what was coming next...or not. Cam's mouth was doing a damn good job of distracting him but even so,

Levi might have jumped when something solid pressed against his ass.

"Just a finger, just one little finger." Cam had big hands. There was nothing little about his finger, but Levi focused on enjoying the smoothness of Cam's neck; the way his mate shivered as he sucked on Cam's earlobe.

"Second finger coming up." Levi wanted to tell Cam not to bother with the running commentary. He was doing his best to ignore what was going on from the waist down, although his cock was begging for attention. He went back to licking the sweat from Cam's skin, nibbling over his mating scar.

Hmm, a drop of his blood would take the edge off, but Levi wanted to wait. Emotions flowed through the blood and the taste would be all the sweeter once Cam was inside of him. Which was going to be soon. Levi winced as a third finger stretched his ass. It didn't hurt. Levi was well versed in what pain felt like. But he felt odd in the pit of his belly and huffed.

"You are too damn tempting for me, babe," Cam said quietly. "Do you think you're ready?"

I was ready ten minutes ago. Levi nodded and then closed his eyes. *Think of something else. Think of how your cock feels when it sinks into your mate's body.*

"Watch me." Levi opened his eyes to see Cam's boring into his. "We don't want any furry incidents."

He'd have to explain to his mate, at some other time, about how his vampire half was holding down his wolf and refusing to let him do anything beyond whimper. Vampires were usually switches – fucking and being fucked, they didn't care. Levi was just glad his wolf side enjoyed a taste of freedom in the woods earlier.

But that wasn't the sort of thing he could bring up now. Despite his mental reservations, his body was open and willing and Cam was taking full advantage. There was a furrow across Cam's brow and his tongue was peeking out of his full lips as he held onto his cock with one hand, bracing his body with the other.

Actually, watching his face isn't a bad idea. Levi ran his hand down to his own cock and gently tugged it as he felt the blunt end of Cam's pushing against his hole. His body resisted, but not for long and Levi arched his back as he felt something like a swollen ball push through his thick muscles to rest on the inside. *Inside!* Levi wasn't going to freak.

"You could try breathing, babe," Cam said with a wince. "Then maybe it wouldn't feel like your body was tugging the head of my dick off."

Long breaths out. Levi knew the routine. He'd had many a man quail at the crucial moment when they tried to accept his length. Huffing and then breathing out, huffing and more breathing out, Levi felt it when his body finally relaxed its strangle hold on Cam's cock.

And Cam clearly felt him relaxing, too. But instead of seeming impatient, as Levi had been in the past with others, Cam's smile widened. "You have no idea how chuffed I am to be the first you trust with your ass."

I do. It's written all over your face, but as Cam started to gently rock into him, Levi relaxed, fascinated by the play of emotions crossing his mate's face. Something Levi had noticed from the first time he'd scented him; how Cam threw himself into every moment, milking it for all it was worth. Just like now. Pleasure, pride, and lust blended with a strong dose of affection. Cam showed it all and Levi couldn't help but respond to that.

He ran his hand over his cock head, collecting the juices and smoothing them down his shaft. Cam swiveled his hips and something electric sparked inside Levi's body. He groaned and then groaned again, because somehow, between the pressure on his cock and the way Cam's stroked that spot inside, he was close to coming. His balls were tight and suddenly Levi needed to come. Not content with lying like a lump, his hips finally moved and that caused Cam to speed up.

He's fucking me into the mattress, and Levi rejoiced in every second of it. He'd never felt so wanted or cherished. Cam hadn't stopped watching his face. Nothing about this fuck was random. It was them, coming together the way all mates should, and as Levi felt his cock spurt he tilted his neck, offering his submission.

Cam growled and struck; his teeth covering Levi's mating mark perfectly. Levi's wolf howled and his vampire cheered. *Fuck, it gets crowded in my head sometimes,* Levi thought as he relaxed back into the mattress. His ass was damp and sticky but his soul was calm.

"Feed," Cam said gently, nudging Levi's face to his neck. "Can't let your vampire side miss out."

Sipping quietly on Cam's neck, Levi wrapped his arms around his mate and held on tight. He was never letting go again.

Chapter Eight

Cam surveyed the new challenge circle and the surrounding stands. He should have felt guilty he and Levi spent the entire previous day in bed, but Kyle and Michael hadn't let him down. The circle was flat and swept clean and Cam could tell without checking it would be regulation size.

The stands were sturdy and constructed out of thick wood, set a decent distance away from the circle. Although, as with anything shifter, they ringed the circle almost completely. Only one stand was set apart from the others, which would be where the Alpha, Alpha Mate, and Enforcers would sit. At the moment, those enforcers consisted entirely of him, the assassins, and Shadow, so Cam wasn't worried about Aiden's safety, although Ranger was.

"I can't see anything here that Ranger could complain about," Levi said, coming to stand next to him. "You've got no high buildings to hide snipers. Aiden will be protected by enough bodies so no one will be able to get to him."

"Ranger still thinks his mate is a precious wallflower that can't cope with the midday sun." Cam laughed as he pulled Levi close. It was Ranger's call, before first light, demanding he check security for the challenges, that pulled the two of them out of bed. "I'm sure Aiden's going mental with Ranger's protective instincts. I'm glad you're not like that with me."

"I am," Levi twisted his face in the facsimile of a smile. "I just know how to hide it better."

"Just as well." Cam tilted his head for a kiss but a sharp cough had him turning around. "Kyle, I'm not sure you've met my mate, Levi." Kyle's eyes widened and his cheeks turned a lovely shade of pink. The assassin tattoo would do that to anyone, although Cam was biased. He thought Levi was the epitome of male perfection. "You've done an amazing job. I transferred your fee through the bank this morning."

"Thank you very much, sir." Kyle tilted his head. "We've had three other job offers that came through while we were working here. This is going to mean a lot to my parents."

"What is your family's situation?" Cam leaned against Levi's chest, enjoying the heat and strength. "Is there anything else the Alpha can help you with?"

Kyle looked at the ground and scuffed the dirt with his boot. Cam noticed they were barely holding together. He felt a flutter of discontent in his belly, sure he wasn't going to like what Kyle would say. "I'm sure the Alpha has enough to do without worrying about our family." Yep, Kyle was on the defensive. *More shit from the ex-alpha,* Cam thought.

"But there is something that does affect the whole town," Kyle continued. "We don't have any medical facilities. My dad," he looked up at the clear blue sky and then back at Cam. "My dad was one of the original enforcers for the current Alpha's grandmother. When the older Mr. Chalmers took over, all the enforcers were fired; no pension, no nothing. My dad tried to get other work; my mom didn't want to move from here. He was working for Northern Construction but he fell through a roof and broke his back. He was unconscious and by the time he was found, he couldn't shift. He hasn't been able to shift or work since."

Cam's heart went out to the young man. Now he was paying attention, he could see Kyle was wearing the same jeans from two days before and while his t-shirt was clean, it was almost transparent. "I am glad you told me. I thought there was a medical facility in town. Are you telling me no one there would treat your father?"

"There's no one there to do the treating." Kyle pointed up the road where the medical building stood starkly modern among the older style shops and houses. "Northern Construction kicked out the staff years ago and uses it as their headquarters."

Frowning, Cam asked. "How many men make up Northern Construction apart from the three bozos already in jail?"

"There was just the three of them in charge – Joe Fontain, his brother Patrick, and his cousin Nyle. Those were the three you got the other night. They also worked as enforcers for Mr. Chalmers. My dad was a contract worker, same as anyone else who worked for the company. Joe said that's why he didn't owe my dad any money to help out after he was hurt."

"Maybe you should have torn their heads off, babe." Cam patted Levi's thigh. "I wish we'd known about this sooner Kyle, but we know about it now and your family will be taken care of. You should be enjoying life at your age. How old are you? Nineteen, twenty?"

"I'm twenty-five, sir. I've been working since I was sixteen."

"The same age as our Alpha, Aiden. You must come up to the house sometime. He'd love to get to know you. I realize the damage done to your father's back is probably permanent now, but there will be a doctor in town by Monday and his first job will be to do all he can to make your father more comfortable."

Cam noticed Kyle's eyes shifting about and mentally thumped himself. "The doctor will be paid from the fund the Alpha has set up to help the people of this town. So, there will be no charge no matter how many visits are required or whatever treatments he needs. The next order of business is to get you into a proper business. I think Northern Construction needs new premises and a new owner. I'll draw up the papers to arrange for that company and any assets associated with it, to be transferred into your name."

"Mine?" Kyle looked panicked and hopeful all at once. "I didn't finish schooling, I don't know how to run a business. I've just been trying to make money to make mom's life easier."

"My friend, Sean, will help you with the business side of things. He's been getting bored." Levi actually smiled and Cam's heart thumped hard. "He's another assassin like me, but believe me, he'd love to help you and your family now we've decided to settle here."

"I don't know what to say." Kyle ran his hand through his blond hair. "I was just trying to help my parents, you know? When my dad got hurt, no one at the pack house would help. We've been living on charity from our neighbors. But times have been tough all over."

"That is something Aiden is aware of and is doing his best to help with. A lot of money and resources were stolen from people like your father and this town. And that's another thing. You said your father was an enforcer. Under council laws, he had a right to a pension if he ever left his position or was laid off. An enforcer position is twenty-four seven and that kind of dedication is always respected in packs." Cam pulled out his phone. "Give me your father's details and I'll make sure he's paid the going rate for pensions, backdated to when he was first laid off."

"But that was years ago. That's a huge amount of money." Cam could tell Kyle was trying to work out how much it might be. A pension was usually eighty percent of a man's wage.

"And it will be in your account this afternoon and he will receive a monthly amount starting from the beginning of next month."

"I don't understand." Kyle looked as if he was going to cry and Cam gave into his urges and stepped forward to give the man a hug.

"You and your dad, your whole family, deserve a lot better than old man Chalmers ever gave you. This is the least we can do. Now," he added slapping Kyle on the back and moving away. "Perhaps you'd like to share the good news with your family. I'll be busy with these enforcer challenges for a couple of hours, but I promise that money will be in your account today."

"You have no idea; this is life changing for all of us." Kyle shook his head and brushed away his tears. Straightening his spine, he said, "Thank you. It's good to know the town will soon be back the way it was when the Alpha's grandmother was alive. My dad remembers her fondly."

"All the more reason for you to come and have a meal with Aiden. He'd love to hear those stories. Now go on, Sean will be in touch later today. Start looking for a new home for Northern Construction – the doctor will need his rooms back. But first, speak to your family. Let them know things will change for the better." Cam made a mental note to ask Sean to go around and see Kyle's family personally. With luck, there would be other things that could be done to make Kyle and his family's life a lot easier.

"You were good with him," Levi said as Kyle tilted his neck and then sprinted off. "I imagine he feels like he's won the lottery today."

"Let's hope he still thinks so when he gets a look at Sean." Cam laughed and turned to face his mate. "I've got to go and supervise check in. I need to run background checks on the outsiders who've applied to take part of the challenges today. Want to come with me?"

"There are strangers in town. I'm not leaving your side for a second." And yes, there was that protective, possessive wolf shifter hybrid Cam was coming to love. Love. At last. He wondered how his staunch mate would handle it when he finally had the guts to tell him. *Perhaps wait until after the challenges are done. My poor mate is stressed enough with strangers around as it is.*

Chapter Nine

Two hours later and Levi felt a prickle of unease run up his neck. The challenges were over. Levi was impressed at just how much work Cam got done. Not only had he run background checks on every person who'd signed up, but he'd also found the time to pull up Kyle's father's employment records and worked out a sizeable sum to deposit into the family account. Cam had taken great pleasure stripping the Fontain men of their assets, under council law, of course, and signing them over to Kyle and his brother Michael. This was all before the challenges even started.

Watching Cam work made Levi realize just how valuable an asset his mate had been to Ranger. There was nothing that man couldn't find on a computer. And he'd proven his strength twice when two different challengers decided they didn't need to go through a beta wolf to get their chance at a well-paying job. They both left sporting large hand marks across their throats and Levi's boot up their ass.

But it wasn't Cam's efforts to protect himself, or the challenges that followed that put Levi's senses on alert. He watched the crowd move off towards town. He and the others were going back to the pack house where the six new enforcers would be sworn in. Cam was talking to Aiden, but despite only being four feet away, Levi had the urge to get closer.

"Are your spidey senses playing up?" Marcus nudged him, Shadow tucked under his arm.

"Yep. Yours?"

"Yep. Keep your mate close and your eyes peeled on the way to the pack house. Pays to trust your instincts when you're in a game like ours."

Levi would have liked to point out that they weren't in the "game" anymore, but Marcus was right. That prickle up his neck had saved his life on more than one occasion. He was glad when Cam finished talking and came over.

"Something worrying you?" Of course, Cam would pick up on the changes in his mood.

"Not sure but Marcus is feeling it too, so it's likely Ranger and Sean will be sensing it as well. Stay close."

Cam simply nodded, but Levi noticed he was watching the road and landscape as they made their way back to the pack house. They'd only just got inside when he heard the sounds of a truck and a large car coming up the driveway. "We've got company," he said although his words were unnecessary. Ranger pulled Aiden close while Sean and Marcus guarded the door through to the hall.

"You guys sit down," Cam nodded at the enforcers. "I'll get the door."

Stop him, Levi's senses screamed at him, but with nothing to back up his worries, Levi watched and fumed as Cam went to the door.

"I'm Councilor Roger Cotton, I wish to speak to the Alpha immediately." A posh voice and a name Levi didn't recognize. Cam explained Dominic was no longer in his council position. Maybe this guy was his replacement. But Levi didn't like the tone being used with his mate.

"My apologies, Councilor," from his vantage point Levi saw Cam tilt his head ever so slightly. "I am afraid the Alpha is busy right now. If you explain why you wish to see him, I will, of course, see to it he is advised as soon as possible."

Aiden had his hand over his mouth, probably to stop himself from laughing out loud but Ranger looked like someone had shit on his favorite boots and Marcus and Sean looked concerned.

"Get out of my way, beta." It seemed the new councilor had an attitude problem. "Your alpha is responsible for absconding with all four of my assassins, I insist on speaking with him immediately."

"If you had said you wanted to speak to the former assassins," Cam said smoothly, "then, of course, that is entirely a different matter. But I am afraid your men will have to stay outside. Surely a full division of guards is a little excessive as council members' protection?"

"A whole division?" Levi mouthed at Marcus who was closest to the window. A quick peek out of the curtains and Marcus nodded. Ranger held out his hands, pointing at the enforcers, and the others, scattering them around the room with the two biggest standing behind Aiden and Ranger.

"Under council by laws," Levi heard Cam say smoothly, "you are allowed two people to accompany you to a meeting with the alpha of any territory. However, I must insist all weapons are left on the porch. Our alpha mate is a stickler for protocol, I am sure you understand."

"I wasn't aware there was an alpha mate," Cotton said as though such a position was a curse. Aiden held Ranger's hand, beaming at him, but the assassins and enforcers were on high alert by the time Cotton and two large men entered the room. Judging by the uniforms the men had been drafted directly from the guard's division. Both captains. Excessive and unusual, as councilmen were usually protected by their own men.

"Alpha Chalmers, my apologies for interrupting your enforcer ceremony but may I present Councilor...."

Cam's introduction was rudely interrupted by Cotton who scowled as he noted all four assassins in the room. "There you are, you lazy dogs. I've got work for all of you and not one of you bastards have bothered to answer my calls."

"Excuse me?" Ranger drew himself up to his full height. "Did you just call the only four assassins in existence 'dogs'?"

"Council dogs, that's what you are." Cotton didn't seem scared at all, which indicated a definite lack of intelligence. "You work for us. I've been over Dominic's records and there's been some serious slacking going on. Not one of you have worked a job in over a month and I demand you return to the council offices immediately."

"We quit," Marcus waved his hand to indicate all four of them. "Three of us found our mates and our fourth is hopeful. This was all explained to the council when Ranger was sent to kill his own mate. We all work and live here now and we're very happy where we are."

"You can't quit." Cotton lost his composure. Watching him, Levi wouldn't be surprised to see him foaming at the mouth. The two guards who came with him were watching the procedures carefully though and Levi would swear one of them had a look of disgust on his face when his eyes hit Cotton. "You have been trained to the highest degree; training that cost the council a fortune, taking years to obtain. You don't have the right to quit."

"And yet we have," Ranger growled. "I made it plain at the last council meeting that none of us would be taking jobs anymore. The assassin program was flawed from the start and none of us intend to have any part of it any longer."

"You all carry the mark." Cotton pointed to Ranger, Marcus, Sean and finally coming to land on Levi. "You belong to us."

"And that mark," Levi broke in quietly, "is one reason why you should really watch your mouth. Did you really think your division would be strong enough to bring in four highly trained assassins, especially when they don't want to go?"

"You never said anything about apprehending assassins, sir," one of the guards said cautiously. "These men are legends. They do untold good works for our community. None of our men will touch them."

"You will do as you're fucking told because that's what you get paid to do." Cotton raged. "These men are mine, you understand. My trained killers and they will be coming with me today whether they like it or not."

"Then you'll be capturing them yourself," the guard said firmly, nodding at his companion. "We answer to the council, not to individual members. Gentlemen, we apologize for the intrusion." Both guards nodded and stalked out of the house.

"Cowards." Cotton watched his back up leave, scorn written all over his face. "No matter. I have the authority of the council behind me and you four have ten minutes to pack your belongings and get out to the car."

"Excuse me, councilor," Cam interrupted. "But what about the mates?"

"Yes," Aiden said stepping forward, a haughty look on his face. "What's going to happen to the assassin mates if you take them as you intend?"

"Bond mates are a dime a dozen, especially ones that look like you." Cotton sneered at Aiden. "I will make it law no assassin will be allowed to take a mate. Any existing mate bond will be broken."

"So, you really intend for the assassins to be treated like caged killers?" Cam scratched his face with his phone. "At least, that's what you seem to be telling the Alpha of the Northern States. You intend to shackle them to council demands, break their matings, and ensure they never have a mate in their life again."

"They were trained to be nothing more than killers." Cotton seemed to ignore the hidden warning about Aiden's status. "I know a lot of our kind get off on the sort of power and prestige that seems to surround their existence, but believe me, I intend to change all of that. These four dogs have been treated like rock stars for long enough. It's time society sees them for who they really are; rabid animals fit for nothing but to hunt and kill."

Levi growled, his fists clenched, his fangs protruding from his jaw. But Cam held up his hand. "And what if the mating bonds are true mates, councilor?" He was still holding his phone. "What do you intend to do then?"

"You two claim to be true mated to assassins?" Cotton sounded incredulous.

"Three of us." Shadow stepped forward to stand by Aiden, twirling a knife in his hand. "All true mates. What do you intend to do with us while your dogs are running around doing your bidding?"

"I will have the matings broken." Cotton spat on the floor. "I know a shaman. It can be done. I won't have my assassins distracted from their work."

"Did you hear that?" Cam asked into the phone. He smiled and nodded and Levi just managed to catch the phone when it was thrown at him.

"Kill him," he recognized the gravelly voice of Tron, his old trainer. "Council orders. Any means necessary. Think of it as your one last job."

"Understood." Levi slipped the phone into his pocket and nodded at his friends before rubbing the spot between his eyes.

"Not on the carpet," Aiden yelled. It seemed Ranger had been telling tales out of school.

"What, what...who was that on the phone? Did you record me? You've got no right. I'm a councilman." Cotton's face went white as all four assassins advanced on him.

"It seems you were right," Levi said, flexing his claws. "We did have one last job to do after all. Who wants to do the honors?"

"Let's take a limb each," Sean cracked his knuckles. "The alpha has ordered us to take him outside."

"Ooh, a tug of war. Come on Aiden, you have to watch this." Shadow clapped his hands.

"You will all stay in here with the new enforcers," Marcus tugged Shadow back and the smaller man pouted. Cotton wasn't given the same option as Levi and Ranger grabbed an arm each, while Marcus and Sean took his legs. The man started screaming before they made it to the door, but he didn't scream for long.

/~/~/~/~/

"Anyone for coffee?" Cam said brightly looking at the enforcers. A couple of the faces had a green tinge, especially when Cotton's screams finally stopped.

"Alpha." A tall blond alpha type addressed Aiden. "Will we be required to work with the assassins as part of our duties?"

"One of those assassins is the alpha mate. Another one is mated to my second. I really don't see it can be avoided, can you?" A flush of red moved up Aiden's neck and Cam could see he was annoyed at what he perceived as an insult. After Cotton's disgusting comments, Cam wasn't surprised Aiden was feeling defensive.

"You will have a unique opportunity in this pack," Cam said, moving so he was in between Aiden and the blond, forcing the questioner to focus on him. "All four assassins form Aiden's inner circle and one of you will be selected, as well. You will all be expected to train with our mates once a week. This will ensure the skills you showed in the challenge ring will stay sharp. It has always been the alpha mate's intention to surround Aiden with only the very best and strongest wolves around."

The blond was paying close attention and Cam chose his next words carefully. "I am sure you will all agree this is a huge honor. No other shifter has ever been allowed to see how the assassins train. It won't be easy, but the rewards in terms of your career and status will be huge. It is your decision, of course, and you are free to leave now if you so wish. However, if you agree to these conditions, then swear loyalty to the Alpha and we'll find you your new rooms."

Aiden threw him a grateful smile, but Cam was watching the enforcers.

Honor and loyalty were the two mainstays of shifter existence. If these guys stepped forward and accepted their position, their personal standing among other wolves would be increased. Of course, none of them would be taught all the assassin tricks of the trade. Ranger would never allow anyone near his mate he personally couldn't beat in a hand to hand combat. But the training they would get would be more than even the council guards went through.

And it seemed the six new recruits were thinking the same thing as one by one, they all sank to their knees, hand over their heart, as they pledged their loyalty to Alpha Aiden Chalmers. The blond was the last one to do it and Cam pulled him aside as the others went to find their new rooms.

"Do you have a problem with assassins?" He asked quietly.

"Hell, no," the blond who Cam remembered was called Paul shook his head. "One of the assassins, I don't know who, saved my sister from a group of rogues. I've always had the deepest respect for them."

"But?"

"The bastards always get the girls, right? Or blokes, if that's what they are into." Paul looked around but no one was paying them any attention. "Ordinary guys like us don't get a look in when they're around. I figured if we was hanging around with them all day, my dick would never get any satisfaction."

"Well, Sean is the only one who's single," Cam laughed. "As I told Cotton, the other three are all true mated, one of them to me. But I know what you mean. Believe it or not, the assassins find it a curse – people throwing themselves at them all the time."

"A curse?" Paul's eyebrows almost disappeared under his hair. "It's my idea of heaven. People coming on to me and begging for my attention."

"It's not all it's cracked up to be. Even mated, Levi still has men and women falling at his feet. Believe me. The novelty doesn't last for long."

Cam could see Paul wasn't convinced. But he went to his room, still shaking his head. Looking around, Cam couldn't see Levi anywhere and decided to go and look for him. Considering an assassin's kill time was roughly thirty seconds, it was high time Levi was back by his side.

Chapter Ten

"He was going to fit us with fucking collars." Levi tugged the offending objects from Cotton's jacket and threw them on the ground. "Look at them. Four of them. Complete with fucking dog tags with our names on them."

"He's got some seriously twisted ideas," Ranger agreed, picking one up. "At least he bought the ones that expand when we shift. Who gave the kill order?"

"Tron." Levi pulled out Cam's phone, finding the call and hitting the call-back button. "Sir, the order has been completed. Now, do you want to tell us what that was all about? How did Cotton even know where we were and what the hell was he doing turning up with a full division of council guards?"

"I'll tell you all over dinner. Expect me at six." The call went dead.

"Tron never was one for chatting on the phone." Marcus picked up the collar with his name on and put it in his pocket. "What do we do with this mess? Usually, the council cleans up after us."

"I don't want to see another fucking council member for the next ten years," Sean growled. "I'll find a fucking shovel."

"I'm going to find Shadow. I'm probably going to get my ass kicked for forcing him to miss out on the fun," Marcus said with a sigh. "You two make sure no one else comes near here. Cotton made a bit of a mess."

Ranger sighed as he parked his butt against the nearest tree. "I won't be sorry to give up this life," he said quietly.

"Because of Aiden?" Levi picked a neighboring tree, mirroring Ranger's pose.

"Not just Aiden. I was sick of it long before he came along. I just didn't have anything else in my life."

"Me neither." Levi thought back over the past twenty years. It wasn't so bad before he scented Cam. He'd do his job, hit the nearest town and do his best to get drunk and find a hook up after. It wasn't ideal, but after spending most of his life alone he used to kid himself he had a purpose. "Do you think Cotton was right? That we are just council killer dogs?"

"It used to feel like it sometimes," Ranger stared at the sky through the tree canopy. "I used to tell myself we were doing some good. We saved the innocent when we could even if we went against council orders to do it. The people we killed were never going to turn their lives around no matter what happened to them. But the bottom line was, there's only so much blood you can have on your hands before you can't get rid of the stench."

Levi looked at his own hands. The blood on them was fresh; it was all Cotton's. But he knew exactly what

Ranger was talking about. "Do you think it will ever fade away?"

"I think having the love of a good man goes a long way towards making it seem less important. I didn't realize how lonely I was until I met Aiden. Before him, I was silly enough to think I preferred my own company. Seems a bit pathetic now."

"That was one of the reasons I left Cam alone even after I scented him," Levi admitted. The blue sky was a brilliant contrast to the greens and yellows of the leaves. "I always felt dirty somehow, no matter how many people threw themselves at me when I went out. I didn't want that dirt to tarnish Cam's light."

"You forget, he's taken a lot of lives himself. He's saved me more times than I can count," Ranger said quietly. "Him and Aiden, I think they were just born that way. Good natured, never letting anything faze them. Personally, I think having someone like that in our lives is like getting a gift from the Fates. A reward for all the horror we've been through."

Levi had never thought about things that way before. He'd never dreamed anything he did in life was worthy of a reward. And yet, Cam accepted him, held him, possibly even loved him, and for the first time in his life, Levi wondered if he could be worthy of that – even love his man in return.

"Did you know I'm a hybrid?" He asked, the summer sun and the blue sky prompting his confession.

"I guessed. No pure wolf could've stayed away from his mate as long as you did."

"It doesn't bother you having a loose cannon in the pack like me?" Levi could still remember the taunts and hatred poured on him when he was younger.

Ranger's eyes met his. "You are who you are. You're one of my brothers from another mother. The day you raise a hand against my mate I'll rip your throat out. But if you're asking if I've ever worried that you would turn against me or the man who means more to me than breathing, then the answer is no. I trust you. Maybe it's time you trusted yourself." He nodded over Levi's head and Levi turned and saw Cam striding through the trees; his perpetual smile on his face.

"God, you guys sure made a mess. Where's the shovel?" Cam's laughter rivaled bird song in its beauty. Levi smirked. His vampire apparently had a poetic side.

"Sean's working that out now," he jumped up and brushed the grass from his ass. "How about we go and find some lunch?"

"We'll stay and keep Ranger company," Cam countered firmly. "You aren't working for the council anymore. That means you clean up your own mess."

For some reason that struck Levi as funny. Tipping his head back, he let out a long laugh, frightening the birds and causing Ranger to raise his eyebrow. Maybe it was simply the fact that Levi finally felt free. Ranger knew his secret and didn't care. Cam knew and pandered to his vampire side. Cotton was dead and Tron said killing him was their last job. Even the knowledge he'd always be marked by that wretched tattoo on his face wasn't enough to quell his happiness. *I am finally free to love.*

Chapter Eleven

Dinner was an interesting affair. Cam had never had a lot to do with Tron, preferring to stay out of his way when Ranger was in training. The enforcers were given the night to acclimatize themselves and get settled into their new rooms. Marcus and Shadow planned to put them through their paces in the morning. So, for now, just the assassins and their mates were at the dining table. Tron's lack of desire for chit-chat must have been contagious as barely anyone said a word beyond "pass the salt, please."

It wasn't until the plates had been cleared away and the men were lingering over coffee that Tron planted his giant-sized elbows on the table and scowled at his former trainees. "You boys have caused me a lot of trouble with the council."

The four men with identical tattoos on their faces looked at each other. Ranger spoke first. "Perhaps you need to be more specific as to what you mean by trouble. Was it because of that shit with Dominic? Because you should know I was prepared to kill him the moment he ordered me to kill my mate. But I didn't lay a hand on him. He was jailed for his own stupidity."

"I'm not saying you did the wrong thing with your mate, although I'll be having words with you, Levi, later." Cam dropped his hand on Levi's knee as he felt his mate flinch. "A mate is a precious gift. You'd have been a lot more efficient if you'd claimed him sooner."

Levi looked as if he wanted to respond but Marcus interceded. "Regardless of what Levi and Ranger did or didn't do with their mates, why are you in trouble with the council? We haven't seen you in months and you had nothing to do with us ending up here."

"You've caused a lot of shit because all of you are in the same place."

Tron thumped the table and the coffee cups all flew up. "I get that you want to be with your mates. You've all worked hard for a long time. Sean basically retired and no one blinked an eyelid about it. No one had a problem with you, Marcus, when you started turning down jobs too dangerous for your mate."

"You did what?" Shadow slapped his mate hard. "We'll be talking about this later."

"You mated an Alpha, Ranger, so it's expected you'd want to stay here," Tron continued, "but did you have to invite all of the assassins to stay in one place?"

"Yes." Ranger looked at Aiden, a warm smile on his face. "Yes, I did. None of us had a home before. Aiden offered us all a chance to have a normal life."

"None of you are normal." Tron was still snarling but Cam wasn't sure why. "That's why you made it through the assassin training in the first place. Because you were loners. Because you had nothing to lose. Now, look at you."

"Now we have plenty to lose," Levi leaned his arms on the table too. "And that makes us stronger and deadlier. Don't forget that."

"And that's what's got the council's knickers in a twist." Tron shook his head. "I thought you guys were smarter than this. How do you think it looks to the council, when all four assassins are enforcers for one alpha, protecting one region above all others?"

"They see us as a threat," Cam whispered, aware everyone heard him.

"Now you, Cam, you always did have smarts and I'm glad to see your mating hasn't stopped you thinking." *Wow, approval from Tron.* Cam wasn't sure the guy even knew his name. He was always just Ranger's sidekick.

"Well, I don't give a damn about the council." Aiden shook off Ranger's arm and stood up, pointing his finger at Tron. "I know you looked out for these men even when you tortured them half to death during your so-called training. But all men, regardless of how they are trained or raised, deserve a home. You couldn't give them that. The council never even bothered to try. My home is open to these men and I don't care what you say or the damn council thinks, these men aren't going anywhere unless it's their choice."

Tron didn't seem bothered by Aiden's confrontational stance but Levi's thigh tensed under Cam's hand. Cam tried to think of what he could say to defuse the situation and Ranger pulled Aiden onto his lap, but it was Tron who responded.

"You'll make a great alpha one day, boy, and with Ranger by your side, I imagine you'll be pretty powerful too as you get older and have more experience under your belt. But this business with Cotton today is just the tip of the iceberg. I've spent the past two weeks trying to smooth things out with the council. Some think you should all be put down like dogs; some want to see you back working the way you were trained to and only a few have come forward and said you've earned your retirement and should be left alone. But all of them agree having all four of you in one place, in one territory, upsets the balance among the four main packs."

We'll have to leave. Cam's heart dropped at the very idea. He hadn't been separated from Ranger since he was a boy. He watched as the four men in question all looked at each other.

"Then we'll take on the council, too," Ranger said finally. "We won't draw first blood, but if they come after us, we'll protect our home and territory.

Marcus, Levi, and Sean are my brothers. We're a family and family don't split up just because some old farts who have no idea of how the real world works feel threatened by our existence. They made us who we are. If we stick together, then hopefully no one else will be made to go through what we went through during the early years. The council ruled our every movement for decades. They are not in a position to tell us where we retire to. You agree with me, don't you precious?"

Ranger looked at Aiden with so much love in his expression it was tangible. Even Tron cleared his throat as Aiden nodded. "You know I consider these guys my brothers too. I'm not kicking them out of their home just because the council, who never did anything for this territory before, says so."

Tron sighed, but Cam noticed he didn't seem surprised. "Well, I hope you've got another spare suite somewhere in this fancy-dancy mansion of yours. My bags are in the car."

"You are staying to help us?" Sean leaned across the table, his claws showing. "You know I respect the fuck out of you, old man, but is there something you haven't told us? Have the council got some ridiculous plan to attack this territory?"

"Nope." Tron tugged on his ear. "Fact of the matter is, the council expects me to drag three of you back to the offices. Their reasoning is that I trained you and am probably the only person left who can reason with you. They accept that Ranger has to stay here. No one would expect the Alpha to leave his territory and they are happy enough with that. The rest of you are expected to go back with me tomorrow."

"You would never betray us like that." Sean shook his head.

"I'm glad you know that, son. Truth be told, I didn't know what I would find when I came here. But after being here, seeing you all interact with each other, hearing what your Alpha has to say. I'd like to be one of those men who deserve a home, if you'll have me."

There was a moment of stunned silence and then Ranger laughed and shook his head. "Tron, you old dog you. If I didn't think you'd cut me open, I'd hug you right now."

"Yeah, let's not get carried away," Tron said, shaking his fist at Ranger. "I'm not the affectionate type."

"Neither was I until I met my mate," Levi's voice was quiet. "I'm glad you're on our side. Consider yourself hugged."

"You can help us train the enforcers," Shadow was laughing now, his bad mood with Marcus apparently forgotten. "Can you imagine their innocent faces when they cop a load of you?"

"They won't be innocent once I've finished with them." Tron flexed his biceps as he stretched. "If you've got no more questions, I could do with some shut-eye. It was a long drive up here."

"Will the council retaliate once they realize we aren't coming back? Cotton had a whole division with him when he turned up." Cam's main skill was strategy and if the territory was going to be invaded by men on council orders he wanted to know about it.

"I spoke to the Captain concerned. He was under orders. He was told Cotton was retrieving vicious rogues from the Northern Territories compound. As soon as he knew it was assassins he was meant to go after, he pulled his men back. The council already know they won't get any help from their guards. There's been a long history of assassins taking on the jobs the guards can't handle. No one in a uniform is going to disrespect that service."

"And economic sanctions won't work because this territory doesn't get any council funding," Aiden added. "I don't see what else they can do."

"The only other thing they could do is declare all assassins rogues," Cam said, thinking out loud. "But they'd have to have proof, so provided you guys keep your noses clean, I can't see how the council could cause us any problems."

"I imagine they will try bribery next," Tron agreed. "For some reason, their losing their hold over their highly trained assassins has got them running around like headless chickens. Don't accept any favor from them for any reason or they will use that hold over you."

"Just as well my baby's rich then." Ranger kissed Aiden lightly on the head. "We don't take their money so we don't have to take their shit."

Cam snuggled close to Levi, his brain still racing a mile a minute. He wanted the Northern States to be a safe place for all four assassins and the people like Kyle and his family who'd lived under tyranny thanks to Aiden's father. He needed to talk to his brother Newton – one of the sharpest legal minds around and the man who kept an eye on all Aiden's business dealings. Aiden might claim the state didn't take anything from the council, but it never hurt to be sure. He was still working out what he could share with his brother when Levi led him upstairs.

Chapter Twelve

"You've got something on your mind and it's got nothing to do with the plans I had for you riding my dick." Levi took Cam gently by the shoulders and stared down at him. He still had to shake himself sometimes; the man he'd dreamed of holding for years was finally right there in front of him. "What is it and what can I do to help?"

"I need to speak to Newton. There is something about this council business that is bothering me."

"Newton?" Levi did his best not to growl but he didn't think he was very successful given the cheeky grin Cam threw at him.

"Newton, my brother Newton; he's a lawyer. He's moved to the Northern States to look after Aiden's affairs. The alpha's inheritance was a bit of a mess and Newton's the best there is."

"I didn't even know you had a brother. I thought...didn't you go through training with Ranger?"

"I was never an assassin, you know that," Cam said gently. Levi found himself herded over to the bed and he sat down with a thump, Cam landing beside him. "Ranger and I ended up in the same orphanage. My parents were lone wolves, killed when I was ten; Newton was eight. We looked after ourselves for a while, but eventually, the guards came looking for my parents' killers and found us instead. Me and Newton were separated. Newton was sent to the Eastern State Orphanage and I was sent to the West."

"Why weren't you allowed to stay together?" Levi couldn't imagine how hard it must have been for the younger Cam. Losing parents would be hard enough but then to be separated from the only family his mate had left.

"Apparently, I was a bad influence on him." Cam shook his head. "Newton was always book smart. When the guards found us, I was covered in blood, trying rather unsuccessfully to gut a rabbit and Newton was pristine clean, reading to me from one of my parent's books.

"You were trying to provide for your brother." Levi was outraged on his mate's behalf.

"They didn't see it that way. If I recall, I was known as the barbarian kid. The separation was hard. We were very close. But being in the East, Newton had access to the finest universities and gained several degrees. I met Ranger. He was the kid no one would sit with at the dinner table. Everyone was shit scared of him even then."

Levi could imagine that. Cam's naturally good nature would have seemed like a ray of sunshine to a boy everyone shunned.

"Anyhow, once Ranger finished his training and we started traveling, I used my computer skills to find Newton and we had a tearful reunion. Then Ranger met Aiden and I was trying to help Aiden gain his rightful inheritance, Newton was the first person I thought of to help. He came, solved the problem and when we moved here he decided to get a house in town. Aiden gave him an office at the bank."

Levi was pleased the brothers had a chance to reconnect, although in his opinion Cam was definitely the smarter brother. Degrees or not, Cam had a keen mind and could apply his knowledge to real life problems. But Levi was struck with a worrying thought. "Does he know about me?"

"No." Cam shook his head sadly. "I told you, I kept my promise. I never told anyone. I was going to introduce you today, but he wasn't at the challenges. But if you're up for it, I'd like to introduce you now."

"You think this issue with the council is that urgent?" Levi trusted Cam's opinion. He had his spidery senses; Cam had years of experience in thinking of the bigger picture.

"I think Tron was given a deadline and while I know he'd never rat us out, I'd like to get someone else's opinion. Newton has worked with the council countless times and hopefully can see anything we might have missed."

In all his years of dreaming of his mate, Levi never imagined he'd have to meet blood relatives. None of the four assassins had any family to speak of, which is why, over the years, they formed their own bonds. *How bad can it be? Twin rogues? Triple vampires or five drunken bear shifters? Newton is one man. A lawyer.* "I'd love to meet him, babe. Shall we take the bike?"

Yeah. He was kidding himself. For a man who never cared what others thought of him, Levi was shit scared one fancy lawyer would disapprove of him. Hopefully, it didn't show on his face.

/~/~/~/~/

Cam hadn't deliberately kept Newton and Levi apart, but the tattoo Levi wore raised a complication Cam didn't want to face. Newton wasn't physically tough, but he wielded words like a deadly sword. When they'd reunited, Newton was hesitant about Cam's relationship with the assassins, but he accepted Ranger was a powerful protector and that the two men were only friends. Mating with an assassin was probably not the type of future Newton saw for him. Then there would also be that sticky question of why Cam hadn't mentioned having a mate before and why Levi hadn't claimed him sooner.

It didn't help that Levi was nervous; not something Cam was used to in any assassin. Oh, they could feel fear; they weren't machines. But with that fear came the confidence of knowing they had a job to do and the skills to complete the work. Levi was out of his comfort zone, Cam realized, and he vowed to trust in the bond he had with his brother and spend his energies helping make Levi feel at ease.

Newton's house was a grand affair on the outskirts of town. Formerly owned by the now deposed bank manager, Newton had taken an instant liking to the large square façade complete with pillars and ornate windows. The door was open when the bike pulled up and Cam jumped off and hugged his brother hard.

"I need your advice, bro. The council could be about to cause problems for this territory," he said quickly as Levi came up behind him. "Say hello to my mate, Levi, and let's head inside. I hope you have the coffee on. Levi takes his black."

"Hold on, just a minute. You're mated. To an assassin?"

"That's what I said. Come on Levi, let's get inside. No need to cause public panic unless we have to." Cam grabbed Levi's arm and tugged him towards the door. Newton followed but his pursed lips indicated Cam wasn't going to be able to distract his brother.

"You've done the place up nice, bro." Cam continued his ramble as he and Levi headed towards the kitchen. "I sent Kyle and Michael the ownership papers for Northern Construction now the bozos who were running it are in jail. If you want anything done, I can highly recommend them. Oh, good. You have the coffee on."

"Cam. Stop." Newton's words froze him in the act of reaching for a coffee mug. "I've heard you talk about Levi before. You know all the assassins and have done for years. Why am I only hearing about your mating now?"

"There were a few complications." Cam did not want to lie to Newton, but he wasn't going to make Levi out like a bad guy either. He'd lived with the 'protect his mate' rule for a long time. "All of the assassins are retired now and living in this pack. Isn't it great? No more traveling." He grabbed two coffee mugs and filled them before setting them on the kitchen table. "Sit down, Levi. Newton won't bite."

"I might if someone doesn't tell me what the hell is going on," Newton snarled as Levi sat down. "Levi. Maybe you can fill me in seeing as my brother's been infected with verbal diarrhea."

"I met your brother eight years ago. I knew we were mates but didn't claim him. I lost control nine months ago and claimed him then and yes, I left him. But as soon as Ranger called us here, I came and begged my mate to give me a chance of being the man he deserves."

Newton crossed his arms and frowned. He shared Cam's coloring but not his bulk. In a freshly pressed polo shirt and tailored pants, he still looked formidable. "There is a hell of a lot more to that story than you're saying, assassin. And if you claimed my brother nine months ago, why am I still hearing rumors about Cam fucking half the men in the Western State?"

Levi growled and Cam quickly intervened. "I promised Levi I would keep our mating a secret. You know damn well I wasn't able to get a hard on for anyone else but my mate from the moment I scented him. But I had a reputation to uphold. I didn't want people to think I was weak because my dick didn't work. It's amazing how many hookups are willing to spend the night in a warm bed, *alone*," he added as Levi growled louder, "and spread rumors about what a great fuck I am because of my association with Ranger. Ranger was never interested so I was the next best thing to boffing an assassin."

"You spent years being celibate simply because your mate was too much of an ass to claim you?" Cam was about to answer it wasn't a hardship, but Newton laid into Levi next. "What about you tall dark, and surly? How did you handle being celibate for eight years?"

"I wasn't." Levi's jaw twitched. "I'm half vampire. If I needed a fuck, my vampire side overwhelmed my wolf side long enough to get off. It was never...."

Cam couldn't listen anymore. In a split second he learned what it really felt like when a heart broke. All those years he consoled himself that Levi was as lonely as he was and now.... "I've got something I have to do," he muttered pushing himself away from the table. "Do not follow me," he snarled as Levi went to get up too. "Don't you dare come after me."

As soon as he was free of the table, Cam ran, stripping his clothes off as he went. He remembered just in time he needed fingers to open the door but by the time he hit the porch he was in his wolf form running like the hounds of hell were after him.

Chapter Thirteen

Levi looked up to see a gun pointed at his face, Newton's furious eyes blazing behind it. "Pull the trigger," he said quietly. "If Cam doesn't come back, I'll be dead in a week. The way I feel right now, you'd be doing me a favor."

"I don't owe you any favors, assassin," Newton snarled. "How could you sit there and blithely tell me and my brother you slept around when you knew he was your mate?"

"You brought it up." Levi leaned back in his chair. "I couldn't lie. Personally, I didn't think it was any of your business, but like so many wolves, all you're concerned about is sexual prowess. Cam's done a lot of good in his life. He's been invaluable to Ranger; one of my reasons for not claiming him which is again, none of your business. He's saved lives, worked hard, kept his promise to me like a loyal mate would, and all you cared about was his reputation; one that wouldn't have been easy to get or maintain. He did all that for me because that's the type of man he is and now because of your stupid questions, he's left me."

Levi was hanging onto his control by a thread. Every time he'd touched someone else, his stomach cursed him. He'd pushed through the act because sometimes just five minutes balls deep in another person could stave off the raging loneliness he'd felt from the moment he realized what Cam could mean to him and he walked away anyway. "Pull the damn trigger," he snarled. "Right between the eyes." He pointed to the spot on his head. "Put a whole clip in there, just to make sure."

"You cheated on your mate. You are using your hybrid status as an excuse, but you cheated on my brother." Newton's hand was steady and the gun never wavered.

"Do you think I don't know that?"

"You said you claimed him nine months ago. How many men did you stick your dick in after that? How many?"

"None. Not one single time. I couldn't. After Cam...." The only reason Levi kept his head upright was because he wanted Newton's shot to hit true. Unless Newton hit the right spot, he'd survive and with his heart in shreds, Levi already knew that wasn't an option without Cam by his side.

He caught Newton's eyes and held them easily. "It wasn't an easy thing to do, even though before claiming him, I could go years without seeing him. I used to dread taking jobs with Ranger because I knew Cam would be there. Every second on the job my wolf would want to claim him; my vampire side fighting him to hold him back. I used to feel as though I was being torn in two. If I'd claimed him he'd have been torn between me and a man who's back he protected. My

173

brother. I didn't even know if he'd accept my vampire side and I kept telling myself Cam would turn away if he knew. I should've known better. That man is a saint and far too good for the likes of me. I've done nothing but hurt him. Pull. That. Trigger."

Eyeball to eyeball, Levi refused to flinch even as he saw first confusion and then resolution in Newton's eyes. Newton's trigger finger twitched and Levi let out a long breath.

"Put the gun down now, Newton." Cam's voice came from behind Levi but he didn't take his eyes off Newton.

"He admitted to cheating on you, he doesn't deserve your heart." It seemed Newton could be a hard ass too for all his fancy clothes.

"He hadn't claimed me then and he had good reasons for keeping his distance. Put the gun DOWN!"

"You spent years hurting because of this asshole. If I'd have known about it sooner I would have hunted him down and killed him myself."

"Then you might as well have killed me too." Cam was so close, Levi could feel his warmth against his shoulders. "Levi has been my life for a very long time. I love you brother and always will but I can't let you hurt my mate."

"He hurt you." Levi watched as Newton's eyes filled with tears. "He spent years hurting you and you never told me."

"Seeing you with a gun now, do you blame me?" Cam chuckled and Levi's heart, the organ that shut down the moment his mate ran out the door, started beating again. "Newt, we're mates. Mates protect each other and even though Levi wasn't with me, he knew I had Ranger to watch out for me. Levi has been my alpha since the moment I caught his scent. My wolf didn't like us being apart, but he accepted it was his alpha's will. I spent years worrying about him. I never stopped and that's why I can't let you hurt him now."

"But he...he...."

"Yes, he did, but I didn't know about it until today and, honestly, I'd have rather not known at all. Levi is with me now. I am claimed by both his wolf and his vampire and he carries my scar. I love him, Newt, and if you pull that trigger then you'd better save a bullet for me."

Levi's eyes widened and he turned in his chair, looking up at his gloriously naked mate. "You love me?"

"Always have." Cam's eyes were sad but his hand was warm and firm on Levi's hair. "As far as I'm concerned what you did before you bit me was your own business. If I thought about you differently, that's simply because I wasn't in full possession of the facts. That was on me, not you. I had no right to be hurt by the things you did before you claimed me."

"You know I didn't touch a soul after our night together."

"I heard you. I just hope that period of time was as hard for you as it was for me."

"It was." Levi rubbed the side of his face on Cam's ribbed abs. "Reliving that night, every night. I was such a fool to walk away."

"At least we agree on something. Is there any chance you'll love me too one day?"

Levi wanted to thump himself for his own stupidity. "I've loved you from the moment you pretended to be asleep when I left you after our first claiming. I knew from that moment you'd always put me first. No one has ever done that before."

Cam's fingers tightened in Levi's hair and seconds later Levi moaned into the harshness of Cam's kiss. His hands flew up to pull Cam closer but the damn chair was in the way. He struggled to stand, but Cam's grip held him firm. The sound of a gunshot broke them apart.

"Nice to know this gun was useful for something," Newton said, eyeing the fresh hole in his ceiling. "If you could put some clothes on bro, maybe we could get to the point of your visit. I've no wish to see you two fucking on my kitchen table. It would put me off my breakfast."

Cam chuckled and Levi felt a burst of happiness swamp his insides. Moments later he and Cam were laughing hysterically while Newton looked on with a disapproving frown.

Chapter Fourteen

"The good news is that nothing in this territory receives any form of council funding. Aiden's father was a control freak and funding requires paperwork and the council keeping tabs on your affairs. Aiden's father never wanted that and besides, he and that bank manager Jenkins were ripping off enough people in town as it was."

"And the bad news?" Cam was dressed, sitting on Levi's lap. The urge to claim his mate all over again was riding him hard, but Newton was right. They did have things to discuss that didn't involve Levi's dick. Or the gun, now safely stowed away. Cam nearly lost his dinner when he saw Newton threatening his mate. Their laughing fit eased the tension, but Cam's wolf eyed Levi's neck in hungry anticipation.

"There is a law they might use against you; well, against the assassins and this territory." Newton tapped the table as he thought. "It was brought out when the four territories were drawn up. The council at the time were worried that one alpha might think his territory wasn't big enough and try to take over another one. It limits the amount of force any one territory can have."

"Like enforcers and guards and things like that?" Cam looked at Levi to see if he'd heard of any such law, but Levi's face was blank.

"Yeah. The council guard was set up at the same time. The reason behind it was the only trained force allowed would be under council orders, not protecting a specific territory. The guards are supposed to protect all shifters."

"That was the theory behind the assassin program too," Levi said quietly. He'd barely said a word since his confession earlier but Cam knew he was paying attention.

"Exactly," Newton agreed. "There were always meant to be more than just four assassins. The original plan was they would be an elite group of at least twenty; individual men who could take out rogues and criminals without involving an entire division. For some reason, it could never gain recruits."

"That might have something to do with the ridiculous facial tattoo Dominic insisted on, not to mention the barbaric training methods." Cam stroked his fingers over the offending mark under Levi's right eye. "The death rate for assassin training is ninety-nine percent. You compare that to guard training which is only fifty percent. Not even the promise of sex on tap is enough to overcome those odds. Even lone wolves would prefer to try for the guards than the assassin program. Last I checked there hasn't been an application for the assassin program in years. Not since the last class got completely wiped out."

"That's not the point. The issue here is whether or not the assassins can still be considered under council control. If they are, then them being here won't be a problem. However, it would mean they would still have to take jobs. The fact that all four assassins retired to the Northern States is going to be the problem. If the alpha of one of the other states lays a complaint with the council claiming the Northern States has too much 'lethal force' under its control, then the council would have to step in."

"Is that a possibility?" Levi asked.

"It would depend on who knows who in the council," Newton explained. "I would have to research what connections, if any, the current council members have with the other states."

"Can we fight that claim if it comes?" Cam asked. "In court, I mean."

"The council owns the court judges. It wouldn't be easy." Newton's fingers were dancing on the table again. "Give me tonight to do some research. I might be able to come up with something. I'll come and speak to you all at the pack house tomorrow. Will that work?"

"It would be hugely helpful," Cam sighed as he slipped off Levi's lap. "Tron is expected back tomorrow with three of the four assassins in tow, including my mate."

"And that's just one more thing in this that doesn't make sense. Why call them back when they know you are all retired. Did you file an application to retire, Levi?"

"I didn't need to." Levi stood and stretched. "Tron told me when he gave the order to kill Cotton, it was my last job. That order came from the council. It's not as though they don't know we've all retired. Ranger made it abundantly clear when Dominic went to jail. As far as he's concerned, the assassin program has been shut down. There's nothing to retire from."

"Then it sounds like some council members are regretting that decision. Leave it with me. I'll have more for you tomorrow." Newton had already pulled out a tablet and was tapping it urgently.

Cam would have preferred more concrete answers now, but he knew if there was anything that could be found, Newton would dig it up. He and Levi were just leaving the kitchen when Newton called out, "Levi?"

"Yep?"

"Welcome to the family."

Cam grinned as Levi blushed. It was time to get his mate home. He had some claiming to do.

/~/~/~/~/

"I know you need to reclaim me, I get it. Just let me get my clothes off first." Levi landed on the bed with an oomph as Cam tackled him. "Lube?" He eyed Cam's claws. "I'll do it." Rolling over to reach for the tube left on the bedside cabinet was a mistake. Levi felt a tug and the sound of ripping denim filled the air. *Damn it,* but his complaints turned to moans as solid hands pulled his butt cheeks apart and a warm, thick tongue lapped at his hole.

That's a new feeling. Shit. Fuck. Too good. Cam growled as Levi tried to pull away and he was sharply tugged back. "Okay, you want to eat my ass. Fine." It was more than fine, but Levi was losing the ability to think let alone form words. He'd managed to get the lube open and his fingers were coated in the stuff, but with Cam's face filling his crease, finding the room to move was difficult. Cam's growls and moans were an audio aphrodisiac and Levi tried wriggling, his cock still caught in the denim.

"Cam. Calm down." He snapped as he felt a fang nick his butt cheek. Cam pulled away, Levi looked over his shoulder. "I know you said you wanted to eat me, but I didn't think you meant literally. Let me get these rags off." He kicked off his boots and tore off the remains of his jeans.

Cam sat back on his heels like a tanned statue. His cock was solid, the head so red it was almost purple. His fangs were down, his wolf flashed in his eyes and there was blood around his claws on his thigh. "I'm lubing up now," Levi showed Cam the tube although from the harsh panting Cam was close to snapping. He'd have to move fast. Working to get himself open wasn't the sort of thing he'd ever done, but Cam's harsh breathing spurred him on. He winced as two fingers went in when he should have started with one, but he made sure there was plenty of lube pushed inside.

"Now, let me do you." He reached out slowly, gently touching Cam's bobbing cock. Unfortunately, he'd barely got his hand around Cam's shaft and the man leaped. He actually freaking leaped at him; growls punctuating the stabs Levi felt at his behind. Wiping his hands quickly on his shirt, Levi cupped Cam's wild face. "I'm here, sweet thing," he said, keeping his voice low. "I'm here. I'm yours. I will be from this moment on. Always. Always yours."

Cam let out a sobbing moan and Levi winced as his thrusts hit home. Fuck. He felt as though there were a dozen papercuts where his ass should be and someone rubbed salt on them. Letting out a long breath, he concentrated on Cam's twisted face. "It's okay, babe, it's okay. I'm not going anywhere."

Levi wasn't sure Cam could hear him. His mate's wolf was pushing for control and Levi did something he'd never done. He surrendered, letting his body go limp – well, most of it. His cock didn't seem to care Cam was trying to ream him a new asshole. His vampire side thrilled at the rough claiming and his wolf...his wolf was asleep; totally unfazed with how Cam was treating them. Levi could see Cam was close and it was tempting to just let the man ride out his frustrations to the inevitable climax. But his gentle hearted mate would be devastated once he got control of himself.

"Calm down," he said softly, trying to keep eye contact. Not an easy thing to do when his head was being shoved up the bed. He arched his head, dropping jerky kisses on Cam's jaw. "I'm right here. I'm yours now. In my heart, I've always been yours. No one's ever touched me like you do. Inside."

Cam's harsh movements softened and Levi swallowed a sigh of relief. "I'm so sorry." Tears trickled down Cam's face unchecked. "I never meant to hurt you."

He made to pull out, but Levi held him close. "You and your wolf have had a lot to put up with over the years. I understand. But you said you loved me and I love you. Claim me with that love, okay?"

"I can do that. I want to do that." The salt of Cam's tears soaked Levi's cheeks as Cam kissed him. Soft and warm; Levi finally closed his eyes. He meant what he said. No one touched his heart like Cam did. Who was he kidding? Cam owned his heart and always had. Levi could spend a lifetime regretting their lost years, all down to his own stupidity and lack of trust.

But he'd far rather focus his mind on what Cam was doing now. How his mate's warm body brushed against his; how Cam's light kisses tickled his facial hair. The way Cam's hands held him as though he was cherished. His cock, which had flagged slightly, was now raging hard and as Cam gently thrust, Levi felt no tension except from the need to climax.

"Bite me," Levi whispered as he tilted his neck. Sharp fangs pierced his flesh easily and Cam groaned around his skin as Levi felt his insides coated with Cam's release. Holding Cam tight against him, Levi shuddered as his orgasm hit. If there were a few tears leaking from the corner of his eyes, Cam never said anything. He simply offered his neck and it was Levi's turn to drink; love flowing with every sip. Wrapped around each other tight, Levi heard a muttered "I love you" as the two men fell asleep. He was fairly sure he managed to say it back although he didn't know if Cam heard him.

Yes, they were going to wake up in a sticky mess in the morning and there was still that issue with the council to resolve. But with Cam in his arms, Levi vowed to protect his mate and his new home with all he could. Cam had kept his promise for years. Levi fully intended to do the same.

Epilogue

Sean stood frowning at the gate of a small house. The structure showed evidence of repairs, but it was in dire need of a paint job. The lawn was freshly mowed and the small gardens edging the footpath was weed free. But it wasn't the state of the house causing Sean's frown. It was the shouting he could hear going on inside. He looked at the address on the piece of paper he was holding and then back towards the house.

"Did you whore yourself out for that business, boy?" The harsh voice could clearly be heard from where Sean was standing. "Suck the alpha's dick, did you?" His second question was punctuated with the sound of a slap.

"Dad, no." The younger voice sounded really upset. "I told you. The second liked the job me and Michael did. I told him what happened to you…."

"You had no right spreading my business with them's that will take it out on me. You made me look bad."

Sean could barely hear a quiet, female murmur, but he could hear the response. "You shut up, woman. As if I don't know what you do to put food on this table every week. I'd rather starve than take charity…."

A small, pleasant faced woman scuttled past the cottage, holding her basket close. "Excuse me, ma'am," Sean asked politely. "Is this the Hyam household?" He pointed to the house which now held sounds of a woman crying.

"Yeah, that'd be Old Man Hyam yelling," the woman shook her head. "He used to be a good man but he's not been the same since the accident. Spends half his time yelling at his wife and kids and the other half down the boozer getting sloshed. Poor Marie, she does what she can and I've never seen two boys work as hard to please him as his two do.

Surprised all of us, those boys didn't leave the day they came of age. The old man might be in a chair but he's mean with his belt."

"I don't want to intrude, but the new alpha sent me over to help Kyle, the older boy. Cam signed over the papers for Northern Construction to him today and made sure his father got the enforcer retirement package he was entitled to. I thought they'd be celebrating."

"The old man wouldn't have seen that as good news. Something happened to him when he had his fall. I reckon he broke his head as well as his back. He spouts outlandish theories, always claiming his wife is out screwing around behind his back for money. What kind of a man would say something like that about his mate?"

"One who needs medical attention," Sean agreed.

"The boys have put up with it for years. You said you're from the alpha, didn't you? One of the inner circle?"

Sean nodded.

"Get them out of there," the woman said quietly, indicating the house with her head. The shouting had started up again. "Me and some of the other women around here have helped as much as we could. A couple of our mates have intervened a time or two as well when things got really bad. But Marie and those boys deserve better. She's working herself to the bone trying to keep a roof over their heads and the boys are just the same. Never put a foot wrong, any of them, but that old man treats them like shit and from the looks of things, he's never going to stop. He's getting worse." She winced as another loud crack filled the air and someone cried out. "Get them out."

"Leave it to me." Sean pulled out his phone as she hurried into the house next door. He hit the second quick dial number. "Marcus. Are you and Shadow busy?"

"Just lazing around thinking about pizza. What do you need?"

"There's some problems at the Hyam's house. Cam's new friend. I need a large SUV and some muscle." He rattled off the address.

"See you in ten." Marcus hung up.

Sean dithered just a moment. His wolf was pacing, eager to get inside the house and he couldn't work out why. In theory, he should wait for back up. For all his criminal background, Shadow was a master negotiator and this wasn't the get in and kill someone job Sean was used to. But the sound of another yell and a woman's sobbing pleas was enough to make him change his mind. No decent wolf treated his family in such a way.

Leaping over the gate, he landed softly and crept up to the house. The wooden door held traces of a heavenly scent; a cock hardening scent and Sean's eyes glowed.

"You will sign over that company to me right now, or I'll put you in a chair just like mine. You hear me?"

Sean's boot crashed through the door. "I hear you and the answer is no!" he roared. His eyes quickly took in the scene. The room was small, but it was clear someone worked hard to keep it clean. A woman sat shivering in the corner of the kitchen, her eyes red with tears and a stark bruise ringed one of them. Old man Hyam had trapped a young man with his chair, his hand raised. Another younger man was peering down the stairs, his face white with fear.

"Get out of my house." Hyam's face was red and blotchy. His beefy arms were barely contained by his ripped t-shirt and his dark hair looked as though it hadn't been brushed in a month. The scent Sean had caught a hint of seconds earlier was stronger now – coming from the young man held against the wall.

"I am here on behalf of Alpha Chalmers." Sean rose to his full height and the boy against the wall whimpered. Good. He'd caught Sean's scent. "You do not want to mess with me."

"I heard about you tattooed freaks living in the pack house," Hyam sneered. "You all think your shit don't stink. Well, this is my house and I'm telling you to get the fuck out. I might not be able to take you, but I know my rights."

"And I know his," Sean pointed at the boy who was watching him with wide eyes. Boy was a relative term. His mate might look young but the helpful woman at the gate said both boys were legally adults. "And hers," the woman was crying in earnest now, her hand covering her mouth. "And his." He pointed to the young man who was creeping down the stairs. "No one has the right to abuse their family in this territory. I don't care if this is your house or that you're in a chair. No one gets to treat their family like that!" His roar had barely echoed around the room when Sean had pulled the boy from Hyam's grip. "I'm Sean. You are?" This close, the boy's scent had sent his wolf into overdrive.

"Kyle Hyam." The boy leaned on him for a moment and then straightened. Sean's wolf howled.

"We have much to talk about later. For now, can you help your mother? You boy, what's your name?" He pointed at the young man on the stairs.

"That's Michael, he doesn't talk much, but he can hear fine," Kyle said as he crossed over to his mother.

Hearing the implied rebuke, Sean lowered his voice. "Michael can you please go back upstairs and pack clothes for the three of you? Just get enough for a few days. We can get the rest later." Michael nodded and disappeared up the stairs.

"Where are we going?" The woman cried looking at her mate. "Who's going to look after George?"

"Mr. Hyam should have thought of things like that before he started knocking you around." Sean kept his voice low as he carefully approached the woman and his mate. "My name is Sean. As you can see, I'm a former assassin." He pointed to the tattoo on his face. "My friends will be arriving in a few minutes. They are going to take you back to the pack house where you will be safe and cared for. Something your mate should have been doing."

"I can't fucking walk," George yelled, spittle landing on his unshaven chin. "What am I expected to do?"

"You don't need working legs to treat your mate with respect." Sean stalked the man in a chair and loomed over him. The man stank and

Sean's wolf recoiled. "You don't use your legs to say please and thank you. Your legs have got nothing to do with having self-respect and caring for the people who care for you."

The man's mouth flapped open, much to Sean's disgust and he quickly continued. "The measure of a man, or wolf for that matter, has nothing to do with what you look like or if you have the use of your arms and legs; it's got everything to do with how you act towards the people around you."

He prodded Hyam on the chest. "I could hear you from outside. So could the neighbors. I heard you call your wife and son whores. For your information, you wife works two jobs. I knew that before I knew who you were, so heaven knows why you act ignorant of the fact. Your son was gifted Northern Construction earlier today because our pack second saw the work your son did on the challenge circle and after hearing about you and the state of business in this town, decided he was man enough, strong enough, and had enough honor to make some serious changes with that company and the way they do business. When you insulted your son you also insulted our second, Cam. Another good man, mated to another assassin. You need to stop bleating about your legs and start working out ways to help your family instead of being their biggest problem."

"You don't know me. You don't know what it's been like," Hyam said bitterly. "My so-called mate runs around all day, never tells me where she's going. And as for this Cam giving my son a company to run. What a joke. A gift for services rendered I call it. That boy has got nothing but a pretty face going for him."

Sean felt his wolf surge forward and his claws scratched the handles of Hyam's chair. "That man you insult as just a pretty face is my mate. The next word that comes out of your mouth had better be sorry."

"Mate?" Mrs. Hyam gasped.

"True mate. Now, about that apology." Sean was so caught up in making sure Hyam's knew he was serious he didn't hear his friends arrive.

"Now, now, Sean. Is that the way to introduce yourself to your new in-laws?" Shadow could find the joke in any situation.

"Help me get these guys back to the pack house. He's staying here." Sean pushed himself away from the chair.

"Domestic violence?" The look Marcus gave Hyam could strip bark from a tree. But his smile for Mrs. Hyam was genuine. "Let me help you, ma'am. Is there anything in particular you need to bring with you to ensure your comfort? The alpha told me you can bring anything you need."

"The alpha told you to do that personally?" Mrs. Hyam seemed surprised.

"Our alpha is nothing like his father, ma'am." Marcus threw Hyam another pointed glare. "I'd like to think the same could be said for the sons in this family."

Marcus and Shadow gathered up Mrs. Hyam and the bags Michael had brought downstairs. Michael never said a word, but he happily followed his mother out to the waiting vehicle.

"Would you like to come with me, or would you be happier traveling with your mom and brother?" Sean's gaze finally rested on his future. Kyle was tall, but lean, with a mop of blond hair and the cutest button nose Sean had ever seen. As much as he longed to hold the man close and live out a few of the fantasies running through his head, he wasn't going to push his young mate, especially after what he had just been through.

But it seems his patience wasn't needed. Within seconds Kyle had run over and Sean felt thin strong arms wrap around his waist. "Thank you, thank you, thank you," Kyle whispered into his chest, hanging on tight. "You have no idea what it's been like."

No. I clearly don't. But Sean wasn't going to force his mate to talk about it when his abuser was still glowering at them from the corner of the room. Picking Kyle up, he strode from the house, stopping only long enough to ensure Mrs. Hyam and Michael were comfortable with his friends before taking Kyle over to his bike. As he started up the bike, he heard the house door slam shut. Hoping that meant a window would open for him and his mate, he opened up the throttle and headed for the pack house; his wolf howling at the way Kyle clung to his back.

The End - Until Next Time.

Did you notice I didn't say "The End" this time? Or rather, I clarified it. I probably should stop using that sentence all together because there is definitely more to come in this series. I was going to focus on the council problems in this book, but Levi and Cam's relationship was more important and for some reason my muse couldn't allow me to finish the book without giving Sean a hope at his HEA. As soon as Kyle popped into my head, I knew he'd make a perfect mate for our last assassin.

If you did enjoy this story, please think about leaving a review. Reviews mean a lot to any author. I know when I am looking at a book by an author new to me, I always check out the reviews first. So, if you did like it, please share your thoughts with others and remember if you have any questions or comments for me personally, all my contact details are at the back of the book.

Hug the one you love.

Lee/Lisa.

Other Books By Lisa Oliver

Please note, I have now marked the books that contain mpreg for those of you who don't like to read those type of stories. Hope that helps ☺

Cloverleah Pack

Book 1 – The Reluctant Wolf – Kane and Shawn

Book 2 – The Runaway Cat – Griff and Diablo

Book 3 – When No Doesn't Cut It – Damien and Scott

Book 3.5 – Never Go Back – Scott and Damien's Trip and a free story about Malacai and Elijah

Book 4 – Calming the Enforcer – Troy and Anton

Book 5 – Getting Close to the Omega – Dean and Matthew

Book 6 – Fae for All – Jax, Aelfric and Fafnir (M/M/M)

Book 7 – Watching Out for Fangs – Josh and Vadim

Book 8 – Tangling with Bears – Tobias, Luke and Kurt (M/M/M)

Book 9 – Angel in Black Leather – Adair and Vassago

Book 9.5 – Scenes from Cloverleah – four short stories featuring the men we've come to love

Book 10 – On The Brink – Teilo, Raff and Nereus (M/M/M)

Book 11 – (as yet untitled) – Marius and (shush, it's a secret) (Coming soon)

The God's Made Me Do It (Cloverleah spin off series)

Get Over It – Madison and Sebastian's story

You've Got to be Kidding – Poseidon and Claude (mpreg)

Bound and Bonded Series

Book One – Don't Touch – Levi and Steel

Book Two – Topping the Dom – Pearson and Dante

Book Three – Total Submission – Kyle and Teric

Book Four – Fighting Fangs – Ace and Devin

Book Five – No Mate of Mine – Roger and Cam

Book Six – Undesirable Mate – Phillip and Kellen

(Yes, there is a spin off series coming and all I can say about that, at this point, is soon, I'm sorry, but it hasn't been forgotten).

Stockton Wolves Series

Book One – Get off My Case – Shane and Dimitri

Book Two – Copping a Lot of Sin – Ben, Sin and Gabriel (M/M/M)

Book Three – Mace's Awakening – Mace and Roan

Book Four – Don't Bite – Trent and Alexi

Book Five – Tell Me the Truth – Captain Reynolds and Nico (mpreg)

Alpha and Omega Series

Book One – The Biker's Omega – Marly and Trent

Book Two – Dance Around the Cop – Zander and Terry

Book 2.5 – Change of Plans - Q and Sully

Book Three – The Artist and His Alpha – Caden and Sean

Book Four – Harder in Heels – Ronan and Asaph

Book 4.5 – A Touch of Spring – Bronson and Harley

The Portrain Pack and Coven

The Power of the Bite – Dax and Zane

The Fangs Between Us – Broz and Van – a Portrain Coven and Pack Prequel (coming soon).

Balance – Angels and Demons

The Viper's Heart – Raziel and Botis

Passion Punched King – Anael and Zagan – (coming soon)

Arrowtown

A Tiger's Tale – Ra and Seth (mpreg)

Snake Snack – Simon and Darwin (mpreg)

NEW Series – City Dragons

Dragon's Heat – Dirk and Jon (mpreg) (coming soon).

Also under the penname Lee Oliver

Northern States Pack Series

Book One – Ranger's End Game – Ranger and Aiden

Book Two – Cam's Promise – Cam and Levi – (You've just read it ☺)

Book Three – Under Sean's Protection – Sean and Kyle – (Coming soon)

Shifter's Uprising Series – Lisa Oliver in conjunction with Thomas J. Oliver

Book One – Uncaged – Carlin and Lucas

Book Two – Fly Free (Coming soon)

[I have purposefully removed the dates my new releases may be due – there are two new series currently under development (the B&B spin off and a new dragon series) and of course a whole host of other books that will be written. Unfortunately, due to real world concerns, I can't promise **when** new titles will be arriving. All I can promise is that I am still writing and new books will be

released as soon as possible. I am
sorry for any inconvenience.]

About the Author

Lisa Oliver had been writing non-fiction books for years when visions of half dressed, buff men started invading her dreams. Unable to resist the lure of her stories, Lisa decided to switch to fiction books, and now stories about her men clamor to get out from under her fingertips.

When Lisa is not writing, she is usually reading with a cup of tea always at hand. Her grown children and grandchildren sometimes try and pry her away from the computer and have found that the best way to do it is to promise her chocolate. Lisa will do anything for chocolate.

Lisa loves to hear from her readers and other writers (I really do, lol). You can catch up with her on any of the social media links below.

Facebook –
http://www.facebook.com/lisaoliverauthor

Official Author page –
https://www.facebook.com/LisaOliverManloveAuthor/

My new private group -
https://www.facebook.com/groups/217413318738434/

(You will need to be familiar with the Cloverleah series to be accepted, or a friend of mine on Facebook, as there are questions to be answered to get into the group. It helps stop the group being invaded by people who monitor and report posts.)

My blog - (http://www.supernaturalsmut.com)

Twitter –
http://www.twitter.com/wisecrone333

Email me directly at yoursintuitively@gmail.com.

Made in the USA
Las Vegas, NV
13 July 2021